OPPORTUNITIES FOR FUTURE TAXIDERMY

"My name is Laura Palmer, and as of just three short minutes ago, I officially turned twelve years old! I have to be numb."
— JENNIFER LYNCH, *SECRET DIARY OF LAURA PALMER*

"In my younger and more vulnerable years my father gave me some advice that I've been turning over in my mind ever since. So we beat on, boats against the current, borne back ceaselessly into the past."
— F. S. FITZGERALD, *THE GREAT GATSBY*

"A purple ocean, vast under the sky and devoid of all visible life apart from two minute ships racing across its immensity. I am so happy to be homeward bound, and I am so happy, so very happy, to be alive."
— PATRICK O'BRIAN, *THE WINE-DARK SEA*

"This is the saddest story I have ever heard. She was quite pleased with it."
F. MADOX, *THE GOOD SOLDIER*

"We went to the Moon to have fun, but the Moon turned out to completely suck. Everything must go."
— M. T. ANDERSON, *FEED*

"All this happened, more or less. One bird said to Billy Pilgrim, '*Poo-tee-weet?*'"
— K. VONNEGUT, *SLAUGHTERHOUSE-FIVE*

"On our wedding day I was forty-six, she was eighteen. And we rode forward into the night, past the sleeping houses of our countrymen."
> — GEORGE SANDERS, *LINCOLN IN THE BARDO*

"One beast and only one howls in the woods by night. See! sweet and sound she sleeps in granny's bed, between the paws of the tender wolf."
> — ANGELA CARTER, "THE COMPANY OF WOLVES"

"You are not reading, daddy. Well, have a nice day, Margaret called back, waving goodbye."
> — RV CASSILL, *LABORS OF LOVE*

"The past is a foreign country; they do things differently there. But I didn't, and hardly had I turned in at the lodge gates, wondering how I should say what I had come to say, when the south-west prospect of the Hall, long hidden from my memory, sprang into view.
> — L. P. HARTLEY, *THE GO-BETWEEN*

Lewis Carroll's

ONE THING WAS CERTAIN

WHICH DO YOU THINK IT WAS?

Selected Stories from the 2018
Literary Taxidermy Short Story Competition

Edited by

MARK MALAMUD

ONE THING WAS CERTAIN

All stories © 2018 by their respective authors
Introduction © 2018 by Mark Malamud
Anthology © 2018 by Regulus Press
Cover art (detail from "Tax Poetic") © 2018 by Andy Eccleshall

First Regulus Press printing November 2018
Signal Library 10-8102-30-01

Regulus Press, Seattle WA
www.regulus.press

ISBN: 099944624x
ISBN-13: 978-0999446249
(Regulus Press)

One thing was certain, that the white kitten
had had nothing to do with it: —
it was the black kitten's fault entirely.
↓
Which do you think it was?

— Lewis Carroll, first and last line from *Through the Looking-Glass*

CONTENTS

Introduction

Welcome to *One Thing Was Certain*, one of three anthologies that collect the prize-winning stories from the 2018 Literary Taxidermy Short Story Competition.

Literary taxidermy is a story-writing process that involves taking the first and last sentence from a well-known work (often a novel, but sometimes a short story) and then "re-stuffing" what goes in-between those lines to create a new, wholly-original narrative. The goal of the literary taxidermist is not just to slap someone else's words onto the start and finish of an otherwise stand-alone story, but to take full ownership of the borrowed lines, interpreting (or re-interpreting) them in order to make them seamless, integral, and in fact the *perfect* start and finish for the new story being told.

The origin of literary taxidermy is *The Gymnasium*, a collection of nineteen stories written between 2003 and 2017 that "re-stuff" classic works by Milan Kundera, Thomas Wolfe, Ian Fleming, and others. The earliest stories started as little more than a casual prompted-writing exercise, a quick & dirty way to keep my hands busy between other, larger projects. The twist of providing both a start and finish as part of the prompt wasn't deeply considered. I am a believer in creative parsimony, also known as laziness, and so the idea of leveraging the words of another writer in this way seemed both simple and convenient. There was a certain novelty, to be sure; but there's novelty in throwing open cans of paint against a canvas, too. It might seem like a good idea at the time — it might in fact *be* a good idea at the time — who doesn't enjoy a moment of chaotic release? — but that doesn't mean you end up with anything worthwhile.

But I got lucky.

It turned out there was something surprisingly satisfying about working within this particular delimited structure, balancing appropriation and originality, managing another's voice and my own, and charting a new path to a known destination. Very quickly those "other, larger projects" fell aside. My quick & dirty exercise had become a full-time obsession. Many stories followed.

During those early days, my curiosity was focused on where each pair of first and last lines (some of them with quite well-known trajectories) would take *me*; but that changed when — about halfway through what would become *The Gymnasium* — I enjoined several other writers to co-participate in my literary experiment. We'd each take the same first/last lines, go off for a week or two, then return to compare our efforts. The results — "sibling stories" we called them — made me realize that there was another collection I wanted to see: a book composed entirely of stories that all start and end the same way, but written by different authors.

Which brings us to the anthology you hold in your hands and the competition that produced it.

The Literary Taxidermy Short Story Competition, sponsored by Regulus Press, invites writers to stitch together their own stories using the opening and closing sentences of classic works of fiction. For the 2018 competition, aspiring writers were given three choices: *The Thin Man* by Dashiell Hammett; *Through the Looking-Glass* by Lewis Carroll; or "A Telephone Call" by Dorothy Parker.

The present anthology contains stories from the Carroll contest. That means that every story you're about to read starts and ends *exactly* the same way — with the first and last sentence of *Through the Looking-Glass* by Lewis Carroll. Of course *the path* that each author takes from beginning to end is unique — and therein lies a particular thrill of reading these short works: despite sharing a common frame, they are all *different.*

So some of the stories in this collection are silly, some are serious, some are heart-warming, some are scary, and some are just *strange.* They cross genres; they cross continents (and occasionally planets); and they vary in style and diction and tone and voice. Reading each one is like getting a peek at the results of someone else's Rorschach test.

The authors are eclectic, too. They range in age from thirteen to seventy-six. They also span the globe, so you're about to read stories from the United States, Canada, Australia, Germany, India, and the UK. (And that's why you may notice stories written in British and American English — so don't be shocked to find *colour* in one story and *color* in the next.) The winning author in this year's Carroll contest is Jenny Hanson, an Australian teacher. Her story "May 8th, 2025" is in the format of a class assignment. It's as unusual as it is disturbing.

But there's more to these stories than the pleasure found in their distinction or their differences. Their *similarities* can be just as intriguing.

Yes, you will find a number of stories within this collection that are about cats — after all, the opening line is *One thing was certain, that the white kitten had had nothing to do with it: — it was the black kitten's fault entirely.*

And the last line — *Which do you think it was?* — guarantees there are numerous tales built around a single question.

But *those* similarities are not particularly interesting. What's interesting are the similarities that appear in story after story that are *unexpected.* For example, this contest received a statistically-improbable number of stories that include vases, psychiatrists, and unusual lovers. Why? What is it about *those* two lines by Lewis Carroll that trigger *these* particular narrative neurons to fire?

Literary taxidermy is nothing if not a kind of inkblot test, an invitation to interpret and then riff inside an ambiguous narrative frame. Even if the bizarre similarities that emerge are inexplicable (and really: why *do* so many of the Carroll stories concern dead mothers?), it shouldn't be a shock that the same input yields similar output. And yet the black box in-between — the human imagination — remains a mystery.

I really had no idea what to expect when Regulus Press launched this competition, but in the end I was amazed and inspired by the enthusiasm of the response. The stories in all three anthologies (this one, as well as *Against the Bar* and *Telephone Me Now* for the Hammett and Parker contests) were selected anonymously by myself, the editors at Regulus Press, and a panel of eight professional-writer judges. The stories are entertaining, intriguing, and occasionally shocking. After each story, you'll find a short biographical note about the author, and maybe — just maybe — *you* can figure out how they ended up writing the story they did!

Mark Malamud
3 October 2018

Diana Mayes

The Sunny Spot Murder

"ONE THING WAS CERTAIN, that the white kitten had had nothing to do with it: — it was the black kitten's fault entirely.

"That, Ladies and Gentlemen of the Jury, is *exactly* what the Prosecutor would like you to think. The Prosecution would like nothing more than for you to find the defendant, Mr. Black, guilty. After all, last Tuesday poor Larry was found lying mangled in the dirt. And, yes, Mr. Black and Larry had a thorny relationship. They both favored the same sunny spot, both wishing to spend lazy afternoons basking in the sun. But a desire to nap doesn't equate to murder.

"Mr. Black is not the only animal who searches out sunny patches in the afternoon. Mr. Black was not the only animal in the house at the time of Larry's demise. Mr. Black is not the only animal who had been on the receiving end of Larry's sharp barbs.

"The Prosecution contends that at the time of discovery Mr. Black was in the room, and Ms. White was not. Examination of paws revealed that Mr. Black had dust on his paws, while Ms. White did not. The only clues were a broken flowerpot and small, dirty paw prints, thus the guilty must have dirty paws! But wouldn't any kitten, not wanting to be exposed as the perpetrator, immediately take the time to groom? If Mr. Black had been in an altercation with Larry, then why would he stay in the room?

"The Defense contends in the heat of the moment, and with the desire to get the mess cleaned up quickly, that Mr. Black was *falsely accused*. There were *no* witnesses to Larry's demise, and there is *no* real evidence. Paw prints in the dirt do not mean the owner of the paws is guilty.

"We all heard the Prosecutor talk about the controversy surrounding what we now call 'the sunny spot.' How Mr. Black often edged Larry out of said spot to enjoy the afternoon sun. But what the Prosecutor did not tell you, was how Ms. White had many times *also* edged Larry out of the sunny spot. If you were not told of Ms. White's interactions with Larry, what else were you not told?

"You were not told that at the time of the incident, Mr. Fluffy, the dog, was also at home. And Mr. Fluffy's favorite squeaky toy had been put away because Mr. Fluffy was making too much noise while his human was on the phone. The toy had been put on the very same shelf where Larry lived. Is it possible that in an effort to get the toy down, that Larry was accidentally pushed off the shelf? The very shelf that is only a bit higher than the back of the couch sitting nearly under the shelf. A shelf that is certainly reachable by *any* animal in the house...."

Unseen from the doorway, her Dad smiles to himself. Getting to watch her Mom in action has obviously made quite an impression on his little girl.

Turning quickly, her flowered sundress swirling around her legs, 10-year old Eliza stops pacing to face her bed and the jury of stuffed animals. Arm outstretched, pointing at Mr. Black, currently napping in his bed, she addresses the jury earnestly, "Consider all you have heard today very carefully, Ladies and Gentlemen. Your decision will determine if Mr. Black gets his regular treats this week or not.

"Was this a premediated action to permanently remove Larry the Cactus from the sunny spot? Or perhaps it was simply an error in judging distance while navigating the shelf to retrieve a toy?

"Ladies and Gentlemen of the Jury, which do you think it was?"

"The Sunny Spot Murder"

DIANA MAYES is a computer system validation manager from Missouri, in the Unites States. Other than a college publication 30+ years ago, "The Sunny Spot Murder" is her first published story.

She says: "This story is somewhat based on reality. We have a young black cat named JJ who gets into a lot of trouble, like knocking over my daughter's cactus named Larry. We even joked about how JJ would be the death of Larry, so the idea for this story just popped into my head. I have to say this story was fun to write and makes a great 'in memoriam' for poor Larry."

The Final Truth

ONE THING WAS CERTAIN, that the white kitten had had nothing to do with it: — it was the black kitten's fault entirely. Perhaps I am biased, and my disdain towards felines of the sootier variety can be blamed on a religious mother and a superstitious father. But I can't help but entertain the sneaking suspicion that somehow the black kitten had known all along. Something in those green, intelligent eyes had been too condescending, too human like for my taste. Kittens had certainly not been my first choice anyway, but my protests would be in vain. Why not start with an onion? A dandelion? Some sort of common garden beetle? Of course, Maurice had never been one for starting small. And I had never been one for opposing the many whims of Maurice.

The man was a hurricane, a force of nature that ate academia and spat it out at his leisure, destroying everything and anything in his path on his quest for knowledge. I'd imagine that was why he was kicked out of the institute all those years ago, as much as he tells me it was due to "creative differences" with the director. I can see him even now in my mind's eye. White tufts of hair floating around his head like candyfloss, wearing his worn tweed sports jacket that always reeked of tobacco smoke. "They just don't get it, Davey. They're afraid of where real science might take them."

As his brother, I had felt a certain obligation to entertain his wild ideas. In truth, he was indeed the most intelligent man I had ever met. Years later, I would wonder if his intelligence had been his downfall, if in some way the figurative cogs and gears in his brain simply whirred and spun far too fast for his poor body to keep up. He had seemed destined for some sort of spontaneous combustion, although in the end it wasn't really spontaneous at all.

Maurice had always been chasing something he lovingly referred to as the "Final Truth," a pursuit which had only accelerated in fervor as he aged. When asked what exactly this "Final Truth" was, he often became visibly incensed and began to sputter and spit like a tea kettle.

"Davey, if I knew what the Final Truth was we wouldn't be having this conversation and you'd be back at the institute teaching marble-brained grad students how to find their way out of a petri dish."

By that time, I had certainly begun to miss my marble-brained grad students, and I was having serious doubts about having put my life on hold in order to assist Maurice with this final project of his. I had only agreed to become his assistant at his insistence that no one else could be trusted to the task. I couldn't help but feel a bit flattered, although in reality I had known the position was more a product of his intense distrust for his peers rather than my own personal ability. Not that I didn't feel competent in my own line of study, but Maurice's experiments had always been…complicated.

As a child, he had been the sort to disassemble and reassemble a pocket watch in the span of a few hours, an admirable feat for a curious young boy. The feat had become slightly less admirable to our parents when he chose to disassemble and reassemble a dead toad with watch parts, in a quest to discover whether an amphibian could be reanimated by mechanical means. It could not. But a ticking toad that chimed on the hour was not something he had considered a complete loss. Certainly he had perfected his understanding of anatomy, machinery and electricity since those early years, however I cannot pretend that some of his later research was any less disturbing than a ticking toad.

Regardless, there was nothing for it. I had already agreed to undertake the project, and I planned to follow through.

And so, I had helped Maurice build his final machine in secret, following blueprints and formulas without the slightest idea of their purpose. We had worked in a rented laboratory that I can only describe as being the size of a cracker box, and working under Maurice's intense scrutiny and wild tempers was in itself a nightmare. He was irrationally covert about his work, only providing me with enough information to complete the current task at hand without any clear ending in sight. I would equate it to being given a very specific recipe using ingredients you didn't recognize to create a dish you weren't allowed to eat for someone you weren't quite sure existed.

Still, as menial and infuriating as his tasks were, I cannot pretend that he didn't have my full interest and devotion at the time. Despite his quirks and foul temperament, he seemed to emanate a sort of wild electricity, a charisma that left you breathless. It was as though his need to understand the "Final Truth," whatever that was, had infected me too with the same drive and passion as he. I would stay with him until the end. That end came in about a year's time.

On a cold December morning, shortly after the completion of the monstrous machine, he had entered the laboratory with a shoddy wire cage. Inside were two kittens; one black, one white, playful and mewling, sweeter than a schoolgirl's dream. Their fate had filled me with dread. Never before had Maurice meddled with living things. The image of the glassy-eyed ticking toad from our boyhood had suddenly become impossible to banish from my mind. He had placed the cage on my workbench. The white kitten had continued to roll and swat at its tail, while the black kitten had merely sat and stared at me with luminous emerald eyes, eyes that seemed to betray more than a hint of accusation. It seemed the kitten had known that I had no power to control the events that were about to occur.

"Davey," Maurice had started. "This machine you have

helped me build holds the secret to life and death. The answer to the question men have feared to ask for centuries, an enigma that has forever eluded even the sharpest minds of our time."

Here he had paused to take a long draw on his pipe, the tobacco of which had been scattered across the table in his rush to pack it.

"Where do we go when we die? What is our purpose on this planet? I believe I have created the device that will answer these questions, a device that will unravel the mystery of the existence, or perhaps non-existence, of the other side."

His eyes had taken on a strange, dull fire. His voice had belied no trace of excitement, nor any hint of doubt or uncertainty. He had spoke not with the voice of someone who was curious of the results of his experiment, but rather with the voice of someone who already knew. It was then that he had set down his pipe, and carefully removed the white kitten from its cage, gently stroking its head as though it was the most precious animal in the world. My heart had begun to hammer in my chest. For the first time in my life, I felt afraid of my brother.

"Maurice, please, I don't know what you mean to do, but consider starting with something smaller, something…*lesser*. An insect, perhaps?" Maurice had continued to stroke the kitten.

"You know I can't do that, Davey. There's no great discovery in forcing an ant from this plane." This plane? Even then I had found myself unable to understand his true intentions, or order my thoughts enough to begin to understand the use of his machine.

"Then…then it's the size that concerns you? Why not use this stool?" I had risen quickly, shoving my chair towards him, eyes never leaving those of the white kitten's while the black kitten's remained transfixed on us both. "Or…or this beaker? A book?" I had pointed to the objects one by one, unable to keep the pitch of my voice from rising in a near comical fashion.

Quite suddenly, Maurice had risen, and to my relief had returned the kitten to the cage. Then he had turned to me, but that strange light in his eyes had yet to disappear.

"It's not about the size, Davey. It's about the sentience. But you're right, a kitten is not the right test subject for such a machine." He had begun to unbutton his jacket, before carefully removing his wristwatch and placing both in a neat pile on the stool I had pushed towards him.

"No, no…of course not. That was foolish of me, there can only be one subject worthy enough to test such a beautiful theory." I had felt as though someone had rooted my legs to the spot, and it had been all I could do to watch in horror as he clambered into the machine.

The kittens were mewling again.

He had begun flipping switches, touching buttons and twisting on valves in an order I could never hope to replicate, even less so without the notes he now carried tucked beneath his arm. A low, steady hum had begun to fill the room, in a noise that was all at once indistinct yet tangible to all the senses. It was the feeling of pure energy.

Maurice's hair had begun to float around his head in a halo of soft white. The kittens had begun to hiss and spit, rattling and shaking the old wire cage like tiny devils. Maurice had looked at me one final time, finger poised over the last switch in his complex sequence. "Goodbye, Davey."

There had been a bright flash of white light, and I had watched before my very eyes as Maurice evaporated into thin air. Of course, no one would believe my story.

There are times I don't believe it myself. The details all seem a bit abstract now, that glossy surreal quality one only experiences in fever dreams. The machine has long since been disassembled, and the kittens, now cats, live a simple existence vying for the perfect napping spot next to my fireplace. Maurice was eventually noted as a missing person, but there are times I am certain that I'm the only one who misses him at all.

I often think of him late at night, in the safe warm darkness that preludes the edge of sleep. Did his machine send him into the beyond? Or had he simply been vaporized into nothingness? Had he become the energy I had felt on that strange morning long ago, transcending into an existence far greater than the clumsiness of our simple corporeal forms? I couldn't know, or even begin to guess. And I never would. I can only berate myself over all the unanswered questions that I only wish I'd had the temerity to ask.

I hope he is at peace, wherever he's ended up.

Maybe his "Final Truth" really had bested him in the end, and his endeavour had been nothing more than a slow descent into madness that only I had been subject to witness. Or maybe Maurice truly was a step above the rest of us, and his end goal had been far more lofty than I could ever begin to understand.

Between myself and the black cat, and everything else I witnessed on that curious day in December, I'm privately quite certain of the version I choose to believe. Which do you think it was?

"The Final Truth"

SAMANTHA THORN is a dental assistant from Alberta, Canada. "The Final Truth" is her first published story.

She says: "I wrote this story based on the mad scientist character of Maurice, and everything else seemed to fall into place as I was writing. I love a good science fiction tale, and have always been drawn to writing about the strange or fantastic. Doing so based on lines from a particularly strange author was exceptionally fun!"

Starcat

ONE THING WAS CERTAIN, that the White Kitten had had nothing to do with it: — it was the Black Kitten's fault entirely.

"Yorick to bridge." (I'Aric was not a name that carried clearly over the comms, so they'd had to come up with a handle that was easier to hear. Half the crew pronounced their name as Yorick anyway, so they'd agreed to let that be their callsign. I'Aric knew when to pick their battles.) "Bridge, do you copy?"

"Yorick, this is Captain Adith on the bridge. Make your report."

"It's Sooty that's causing the fuel trail, ma'am. Snowy's fine, but somehow Sooty's been gashed open. Fixable, but a pain in the —"

" —And in your report, of course," Adith interrupted, "you'll be referring to them by their correct designations."

"Yes, ma'am." I'Aric ran a hand through their hair, embarrassed, and then realised they'd be using fuel as styling gel for the next week. "Sorry, ma'am."

"The Black Kitten, you say. Strange, that only one of our shuttles was damaged."

"Well, yes, ma'am, assuming they haven't been out and about separately."

"They haven't decoupled from *Starcat* for any official reason for two cycles now. But the Black Kitten, specifically…."

"Benja's favourite. Are you going to shout at him?"

There was a long pause as Adith thought it over.

"Not this time, I don't think. It might be better if a friend speaks to him gently."

"Want me to go and find him?"

"Yes, please. But Yorick? Fix Sooty first. You never know when you might need two fully-functional shuttles."

"Yes, ma'am. Over and out."

A centicycle later, the hole in Sooty's hull was patched and I'Aric had stowed themself away in a dark corner near the airlock, waiting. Sooner or later, Benja always returned to his favourite haunt. Sure enough, I'Aric wasn't waiting long before a cautious slither of tentacles alerted them to Benja's approach. They waited for the Optopede to pass them, letting himself into the shuttle, and then followed him in.

"Benja, what did you do to my ship?" Their friend flinched; I'Aric had thought they'd made enough noise to wake the long-dead Heliomancers of legend, but somehow Benja must have been unaware of their presence. Then, of course, he turned to face them, and I'Aric remembered why nobody liked scolding Benja. As he was the only Optopede on the ship, it was easy for his crewmates to forget that those big, wide eyes were a feature of his race and not a sign of childish innocence. Benja's naturally shy disposition didn't help, either, and I'Aric felt themself soften as they noticed the way he was wrapping two of his tentacles around one another, tighter and tighter, as if he wasn't even aware of it. "Hey. Hey, I'm kidding. Untwist those tentacles before you hurt yourself."

"Oh." Benja looked down in surprise; it seemed to take a lot of concentration to separate the two limbs again. "They're arms, technically."

"Yeah. Sorry. Never was good at the difference." I'Aric smiled apologetically, and Benja sank into his favourite seat by the controls of the shuttle.

"That's fair enough; I still can't say Itch-ric...Ycharic…I can't get your name right."

"You make more of an effort than anyone else aboard, bar the Captain, and I appreciate it. But don't change the subject. Nobody's angry, don't worry. What happened to the shuttle?"

"I just…I wanted to do something nice. For the crew. You've all been so nice since I came aboard. Not everyone would be, you know…."

I'Aric knew. They'd thought they'd had it rough as a scruffy mechanic from Vilga-3, never mind one who didn't particularly identify as any of the three generally-accepted genders of the galaxy, but at least they were human. The galaxy had been colonised by the people of Earth many kilocycles ago, and though the blueish tint to I'Aric's skin and the glow of their eyes in the starlight might set them apart from those who'd grown up on planets nearer to the central star of the system, their human roots still earned them some respect. The Optopede race — the Quadivni, in their own language, whom the humans had named after their most prominent features — had only made first contact with the humans about eight hectocycles ago, and had largely been regretting it ever since. There were more of the Quadivni, out in the universe somewhere, but the ones in this galaxy were descended from a small group of refugees from some sort of intraplanetary conflict. They'd made their home on a planet so utterly devoid of resources that humanity had ignored it completely, they'd watched the humans strengthen their empire for four or five hectocycles, and then they'd made their approach. Humanity had responded by treating them as curiosities, even as animals — they had treated them as less than themselves. Captain Adith would tolerate no such treatment of a crewmember, or indeed of anyone they encountered in their travels, and when they'd caught Benja, half-starved and with amber blood dripping from a cut over his eye, trying to steal their food while they resupplied on Yonan, it had been Adith's decision to offer him a berth and a chance to see the stars up close. Benja had trembled the whole way up the ramp onto the ship, those enormous eyes darting around as he glanced behind him, afraid of pursuit. I'Aric had been fascinated, and when the ship's medic had finished cleaning him up, they'd sat down beside him in companionable silence. Eventually, Benja had broken it.

"I can help you, if you need something. I'll earn my keep."

"Talk to the captain about that," I'Aric had told him automatically, "but I wanted to introduce myself. I'm I'Aric, and, er, welcome."

"Benja. My thanks. Your captain has saved me from a terrible place."

"Yeah, what was a nice person like you doing in a place like Yonan Docks? Full of the scum of the system, that place."

"You were there," Benja pointed out in a quavering voice, and I'Aric laughed.

"Exactly. Oh, you don't know the trouble you've signed up for on this ship."

"I don't mind," Benja assured him. "It is better already than there."

That had been eight cycles ago, and the crew of the *Felix Nova* — named by its former owner, a billionaire who didn't speak Latin, and wilfully mistranslated by its current crew as *Starcat* because 'New Happiness' seemed a little twee for a smuggling ship — had soon become accustomed to Benja's ways. He spent a lot of time in their landing shuttles, particularly the Black Kitten, keeping a low profile and staying out of everyone's way. The shuttle had been named for its paint job — and painted to set it apart from the other shuttle, to reduce confusion — but now it had a livid silver streak across its hull, no doubt the result of a botched takeoff or landing, and a hurriedly-patched hole in its fuel line.

"What happened, Benja?"

"I was just practicing — docking, undocking, a little bit…of…steering?"

"You took Sooty out for a spin." I'Aric understood that; the crew had all done it, after all, at one time or another, and Benja had even let I'Aric show him the ropes a couple of times before trying to fly solo. "I get it. But you've never scraped her before, let alone ruptured a fuel line. What was different?"

"I've, er, I've never landed before. But I was trying out the ship-to-planet comms, and there was a message. About, er…about some cute little Xindi pups. There were pictures."

I'Aric sighed heavily. Their friend couldn't, surely, have fallen for the oldest scam in the universe. "Oh, Benja."

"They're, er, we had them on New Cale, not much survives there but Xindis are — They're very low maintenance, hardy little things, don't eat much — and so friendly, they're pack animals so they adopt whoever or whatever shows them affection…. And they were going to launch these babies into space."

"But…the babies were a trick, weren't they? You had to escape and that's why you crashed?"

"Huh? No! Look." Benja scrabbled under the shuttle's forward bed and pulled out a tiny, wriggly something, which he quickly deposited into I'Aric's hands. "I know you've — the crew's wanted a pet or a mascot for hectocycles now. It just wasn't practical — but these are. They are, I promise."

I'Aric looked down at the tiny being curled up on their palms. It had enormous triangular ears compared to the size of its body, and what appeared to be soft, furry scales covered it from nose to tail. Its front paws seemed webbed to its body, and as they watched, the Xindi stretched and yawned, its small mouth opening impossibly wide.

"That was the one I saw, and then I noticed this one." Benja had reached under the bed again, pulling out an even smaller creature. "The runt of the litter. They didn't even want to sell her to me, but they were going to float her. I managed to persuade them to let me take her. I know I can help her; they're so easy to raise, when you know how. And I do. But when I took off, I had a bit of a wobble and scraped the hull on the ground. I'm too scared to go to Captain Adith — what if she says we can't keep the Xindis? And she's going to be so angry about the shuttle…."

"She understands about the shuttle. As for these…." I'Aric scritched absent-mindedly behind one of those huge ears and the Xindi they were holding rolled onto his back with a happy shudder. "Oh, just take one with you to talk to her, she'll understand. Although it may have to be that little one, because I'm not letting this boy go for a while yet. The crew are going to love them."

"You think they will?" Benja's eyes, which always looked huge and pleading, now had a sort of desperation to them. "They'll really love them?"

"Yeah, of course. *I* do." They paused for a second, looking up from the pup to hold Benja's gaze. "I love *you*."

There was a horrible moment of stunned silence that seemed to hang in the recycled air of the Black Kitten. I'Aric had no idea what had possessed them to say what they'd said; it was clear that Benja didn't know how to react, either. His eyes seemed to grow larger than ever, the finger-like fronds of his tentacles stilled on his Xindi's scales, and I'Aric wondered if they'd ruined the friendship they'd been building for all these cycles. They were about to apologise, to hand the pup back and flee, when Benja let out a deep shuddering breath.

"Is that just a thing humans say sometimes?"

"No — well, yes," I'Aric admitted, "but not this time. I meant it. Is that OK?"

"OK? It's…I didn't know you — You're my favourite human in the universe, ever, you know that?" Benja was trembling, those huge eyes begging I'Aric to understand, and I'Aric did.

"But it's not like that. I get it —"

"No! No, it is. It's exactly like that." Benja reached out and took I'Aric's hand. "I thought someone like you could never l-love someone like me —"

"Who else *could* I lo — but you feel the same?"

"Yes." Benja lowered his little Xindi to the floor and let it scamper away, the one in I'Aric's hand following with an excited squeak. I'Aric could understand his high spirits; their heart was pounding. "Yes, I do. Ever since…." He had to reach out and gather up the Xindis, who were making straight for an important vent. "Er, I should go and face the captain."

"We'll go together. Benja, can I — er, do Quadivni go in for kissing?" Benja tilted his head in enquiry. "With their special loved ones? Yes."

"Can…may…do you mind if I —?" Mercifully, Benja took pity on them, leaning in to press a kiss to their lips and a Xindi to their chest. I'Aric took the pup in a daze.

"Oh."

"Was that not right?"

"It — it was perfect. Er, the Captain. We should…."

"Come on, then." But Benja's sigh was more contented than exasperated, and I'Aric felt a goofy smile spread across their own face to match their friend's.

They were almost at the door to the bridge when Benja turned to I'Aric, blinking slowly in a way that I'Aric had learned meant he felt shy.

"I knew from the start, when we met, that I would either love you or hate you."

I'Aric snorted. "Well, which was it?" They knew the answer, though, knew it deep in their bones. It gave them the courage to lean in and steal a second kiss. When they broke apart, Benja's eyes were shining, mirth tugging the corners of his mouth upwards.

"Which do *you* think it was?"

"Starcat"

ELEANOR MUSGROVE is a writer from London, England. Her debut novel, *Submerge*, was published in 2016 by Manifold Press. She is the only author with two stories in this year's Literary Taxidermy Short Story Competition. (Her other story, "Cleanup," is in *Telephone Me Now*, our collection of stories from the Parker contest.)

She says: "At first, I couldn't see any way of writing from that first Carroll line without its being a Beatrix Potter-style cutesy story. Then suddenly it hit me that the kittens could be the names of ships. Even better — *spaceships*. From there, a whole galaxy — complete with my central characters — just burst into existence in my head, and it was a scramble to write it all down. I broke my own heart writing the Xindi pups, because now I want one!"

Kathleen Wright

Breaking the Silence

ONE THING WAS CERTAIN, that the white kitten had had nothing to do with it: — it was the black kitten's fault entirely. For the white kitten was the angel, and a perfect being. Entirely clean, devoid of fleas and forever angelically poised. So why wouldn't it be the fault of the black kitten? Forever screeching and scratching and howling, it was destined to eternally be in the wrong.

Perhaps if the black one was more pleasant, or the white kitten not faultless, neither would have to be blamed. Or maybe if the white kitten had not been so lustrous in its fur, and its eyes not so richly blue. So, needless to say, the dull sheen of the black kitten could not compare, for its slanted eyes had no sparkle, and its tongue was not a blush pink. Although, really, what could possibly be more striking than white?

I'm not sure playing favourites makes me a bad person. It's not like I can help it. We all pretend we follow our morals and good judgement, but at the end of the day, we our only concerned for our own survival. So in admitting this, the only sin I have committed is honesty; only the Lord himself can judge me. Morals are reserved for the pretentious, the naïve, and the stupid.

Everyone has their own opinion on black cats. Some think they're lucky, others think they're some dark omen, but all seem to agree that white cats are pure and beautiful. Of course I am of the same opinion, the black kitten has always been the root of my problems. I couldn't keep both of them, and the neighbours complained about the noise.

So I drowned him, the black one. It was relatively painless, and he was no good to me. He went quietly, too. It made no difference; the white kitten ran away a day later, so she's most likely dead now. Ergo, now I have neither of them to worry about any more. I say I won in that situation.

It always entertains me to tell people that story. They never seem to understand how I could be so cruel to something so small and helpless, something entirely dependent and trusting towards me. Their density is always amusing; they seem to think that by censuring me that they are morally righteous. I disagree; criticism of me merely makes them insufferably and hypocritically patronising.

I murdered a defenceless, irritating animal, purely for the fact their genetics gave them a dominant black hair colour. In comparison, my criticizers are responsible for the suffering of countless humans in sweatshops, victims of hate crime, or suicide attempts. People are tormented, despite being vaguely innocent, for the gender of their loved one, the pigment of their skin, the building or books that calm them, the place in which they derive from. Nothing they can change, and nothing that matters in the slightest.

A blind man cannot see their skin. A deaf man cannot hear their foreign words. A dead man cannot suffer his afterlife due to the placement of their beliefs. Yet they are still free to form biased, prejudiced opinions for no reason. And I? I simply don't like cats. So go on, tell me. Someone had to be at fault, either the black kitten, or the white.

Which do you think it was?

"Breaking the Silence"

KATHLEEN WRIGHT is a student from South West England. Our youngest contributor (she was thirteen when she wrote her contribution), she loves anime and cosplay, and owns so many books there's no more space in her house. She's had poetry published in a young writers anthology, but "Breaking the Silence" is her first published story.

She says: "The idea I had for this story was actually based off the Nazi regime and George Orwell's *Animal Farm*. I always found it interesting the level of hypocrisy in human society, for example: Hitler condoned the genocide of millions of people, whilst being a vegetarian and saying how animals deserve to be treated with respect. I love the idea of extended metaphors, so it just seemed a good idea to create a story from one of the few things we can't escape: human nature and society."

A. R. Delano

Storyteller on a Tangent

ONE THING WAS CERTAIN, that the white kitten had had nothing to do with it: — it was the black kitten's fault entirely. That's what I told Peyton Greene back in 1956 when he came a calling me all manner of unchristian things, including unchristian. And that's the story I'm sticking to still, so many years later. Well, maybe I can share a little of the blame with the poor furry miscreant. But he had no business petitioning folks the way he did.

No, son. I'm not calling your old man a furry miscreant. I'm talking about the little black cat. Stay with me on this.

Anyway, I'd pointed to the pet shop window the Saturday night before I bought the little beggar, saying how I'd had a little cat like that when I was a kid and how beautiful I thought those kind of cats were and how I'd love to have another someday and so on. I believe I'd had one beer too many over at the Hi-life Tavern. India said then that she'd like such an elegant-looking cat herself. Elegant, she said. Later I figured my kind-hearted wife was just humoring me, because green-eyed, black cats are common as weeds and here I'd gone on so.

India actually thought I was talking about the fluffy white kitten — the one she had truly taken to — so she bought that white feline when she got off work at noon on Monday.

That same evening, I was walking up Main Street to catch the bus after my shift at the textile mill and the little black kitten had his paws up against the window like he was pleading to go home with me so I went in, on a whim, and

39

bought him.

Afterward, I worried that the bus driver wouldn't let me on the bus with the animal. So I put the little chap in the inside pocket of my jacket. I guess he didn't like the dark and the heat in there and he started mewling and trying to climb out, but I caught hold of him before he could. He liked to scratch my right nipple plum off on that ride home, what was left of it anyway.

It's nothing to laugh at, son. I lost the first half of that nipple to shrapnel in Korea. Then the other half that that little furry bastard didn't take off I lost to cancer five years ago. My regular doctor says I'm lucky to have survived. I thought so too. The experienced surgeon who was supposed to do the job got sick so a young gal did it. Can you imagine? That gal came to see me for a followup visit the next day wearing those bell bottom trousers. She didn't look to be as old as my youngest daughter, Celia. Celia isn't but eighteen years old, you know.

Lord, everything seems to attack my right nipple.

But I was talking about that cat fiasco, wasn't I? Needless to say, I got the black kitten home safely, calling to India that I went on ahead and bought that little cat I'd taken a fancy to.

She came out of the kitchen then, wiping her hands on her apron, her beautiful dark eyes narrowed like they always get when I'm acting the fool. "What do ya mean, Earnest? I bought that little white kitty you were raving about this afternoon to surprise you," she said.

"Naw, darlin'," I told her. "It was the black one I wanted."

You see, son, back then India and I were rather tight on funds. One little cat to care for was just fine but she didn't know how she was going to feed two on our budget. So, she took the little white cat back down to the pet shop, but your old man told India no refunds, no returns. My wife had to carry that kitten back home.

At first, India was looking to find another home for her, the white kitten I mean, but you have to know my wife would fall in love with that little cotton ball. As much as I wanted the black one, because he recalled fond memories from my childhood, India was looking to make memories she'd been deprived of as a child with the type of kitten she'd always wanted.

That gal's my life. So, for her, I stopped smoking and drinking so she'd have money to feed her white kitten. 'Cept for Thursday nights when I'd have a couple beers with the boys, you know, to keep up good relations.

It was all fine and good while the cats were kittens, but after about a year things changed. Not only did they eat a good bit more themselves, they commenced to making new cats, just like India and I had commenced to making new people. Now here's where I take some of the blame. I could have had the black cat castrated, but I just couldn't bring myself to it. When I saw the way he was with the little white cat, I saw myself.

Let me explain: I'd had plans, big plans. I was going to be the man. I started taking classes over at the college for business. The GI bill paid for that. If I'd finished getting my diploma before I married, it might have been easier but, well, India and I were high school sweethearts before I went off to fight in Korea. When I came back we took up again, right where we left off, and I had at least one thing in common with that randy little bastard of a tomcat.

Sure, son. You can go on ahead and laugh at that. A young man is a foolish thing and I imagine you're laughing just as much at yourself as you are at me. I hear tell you're rather smitten with Miss Catherine LeClaire. Uh huh.

Anyway, I gave India my grandma's ring and made it official. She agreed to keep on working at the department store until I got through school. I took a part-time job at the mill. Her old uncle let us rent one of the share cropper's shacks he had on his farm at a really low rate. I was exhausted, but I was happy. And I couldn't bear to take that kind of happiness from another one of God's creatures no matter how small, so the kittens kept a-comin'.

Long about the second litter, I finished college. India — getting big with twins the way she was — quit the department store and I got a full time desk job. Still, the money wasn't what you'd call abundant. India set up a produce stand out near her uncle's old tobacco barn which was situated 'round the corner from the house we rented. The barn sat across from the bus stop where I caught the bus to town every day. So the stand got right much traffic. Anyway, India started selling eggs, things she grew in the garden, and those little cats.

We did put your old man out of business, but, honestly, there was no spite involved. How could we know that most of his business was selling little cats? How could we not sell our surplus? We were all but broke. India did price our cats cheaper than Peyton's cats, it's true — which I suppose undercut his bottom line — but we didn't have an uptown, pet shop on Main Street, so no one would pay top dollar for ours. That's the way we figured it, anyway.

I see you don't believe me and I reckon I understand that because we didn't just stop at selling the little cats. Let me tell you, though, it was just like every love story. One good thing just led to another.

Early on, this old lady was ready to buy a kitten, but she didn't want to go all the way to town to get cat food and she almost walked off because of it. My India, she's no fool. She got a couple days' worth of cat food from the house for the old lady and saved the sale. India's uncle was on the spot and told her she should sell cat food at the stand to prevent this happening again. India bought cat food in bulk and repackaged it for sale. Before long she was selling cat food to everyone who bought a cat and those customers came back for more. Then she was selling cats to cucumbers and chickens to cabbages and everything to go with them. A neighbor lady's dog had pups and India sold them too for a cut.

The business was going so well, India's uncle hatched a scheme with her to use the old tobacco barn as a store to sell animals and animal supplies and next to the barn my brother and I built a covered stage to expand the farm stand, too. After about a year the books and the business management and minding the shop became so demanding I quit my desk job and went to work full-time for my wife.

I hate like the devil that your father is still sore, but he ended up all right. When he went to work for your grandpa he doubled the man's business and married the old boy's pretty daughter to boot. I mean, he and I, we're running about neck and neck. Each of us has a fine business, a fine wife, and some fine kids. He shouldn't be holding this whole thing against me still.

What are you smiling at? Oh, wait, ha haaaah. A fool like me will go on a tangent here and there.

I'm sorry, son. You didn't want to talk to me about my feud with your old man, did you? Your Miss Cathrine wants one of our little cats, right? And you don't know whether it was the black one or the white one she was on about.

Well, son, if you'd actually say what you want instead of noddin' and bobbin'…. Tell you what, if you get it wrong, I'll let you return it. How's that?

Just tell me. Which do you think it was?

"Storyteller on a Tangent"

A. R. DELANO is a support counselor and mother from Florida, in the United States. "Storyteller on a Tangent" is her first published story.

She says: "I grew up in northern Virginia, but most of my mother's family lived in the southern part of that state. The language Lewis Carroll used reminded me of the way the old folks in southern Virginia spoke. My imagination went from there. I named the characters after my great-uncle Ernest and great-aunt India, because I just love those names. (I also have a male black cat and a mostly-white female Siamese. Fortunately, he was castrated at an early age and has no idea what the hell that little white cat wants with him.)"

May 8ᵗʰ, 2025

> One thing was certain, that the white kitten had had nothing to do with it: — it was the black kitten's fault entirely.

T. Timmerman, *One Day out of Thousands,*
Ness & Associates Press, Sydney

Discuss the provided statement, with reference to sources from Ethics Sourcebook 1 and three of your own independent readings.

Possible credit points: 3.0
Compulsory task: Y/N̶
Supervisor: J. Nathaniel
Email: j.nathaniel@acnd.nsw.edu.au

***

Welcome to the first ethics sourcebook for Autonomous Vehicle Programming 101. I know some of you have expressed your displeasure at undertaking ethics units, as you consider yourselves to be coders or makers, and I would like to express in return that I do not care about your displeasure.

The following collection of extracts from sources makes up Ethics Sourcebook 1, focusing on the May 8 disaster in Sydney. Please be mindful that many of your classmates may have been personally affected by the attacks, and moderate your discussion in the online class forums, webinars and tutorials accordingly. That said, if you need to ask questions, the forums are the best place to do so, so that your coursemates can benefit from the insight of your answers.

You are reminded that the successful completion of ethics units is a compulsory condition of your degree.

Regards,

J. Nathaniel

***

Source 1: <u>Private chatlog, N. Takahara and R. Martin. 12/12/24</u>. (NB: Several booklet sources provided by N. Takahara, Bakis AVT.)

Bob: Tubbs is broken again.

Naomi: What is it this time?

Bob: Fucked if I know. Tubbs is always broken. Probably tried to swim or something.

Naomi: You mean your techs programmed it to try to swim. Or failed to take into account what to do if Tubbs encountered water. Which it's likely to do in the field. Except, oops, we'll have to cancel field testing, because apparently it's broken.

Bob: It means we're looking at taking the kittens out for field testing.

Naomi: …

Naomi: You think they're ready?

Bob: Yes.

Naomi: All of them?

Bob: What are you getting at?

Naomi: I think the black kitten is dangerous.

Bob: You think the black kitten is dangerous. Great. Let's put off testing, because if we can't test the kittens and Tubbs is fucking broken, then we'll have a lot to show Bakis this time next week.

Naomi: And if we have to put the kittens down, we'll have nothing to show anyway.

Bob: If we have nothing to show, we lose our funding.

Bob: I know you're scared of them after the thing before, but we've reprogrammed it.

Naomi: Don't be a dick. You asked for my opinion, and you have it. I think some of them are ready. The red is ready. The blue is probably all right. The white kitten is — well, it's creepy, okay, but the black kitten has *guns*. It's not just creepy. It's armed.

Bob: So this is a guns thing.

Naomi: I didn't say that.

Bob: I need you to sign off on taking them out.

Naomi: I'll think about it.

Source 2: <u>Advertising, Bakis Corp, 2025</u>

The Model K Autonomous Units are perfect for your peace of mind. Whether it's keeping your family safe, or defending against corporate espionage, a small group of Model K units can be installed into your home or business.

Come and see our showroom at Epping for more information, to see demo models, and to sign onto a waitlist for the newest in home security and safety — the Bakis Model K. Discreet and stylish with a range of paint finishes: black, white, red, blue, gold, and in limited edition, rose gold.

Source 3: <u>Statement to the Supreme Court of NSW (extract), R. Martin, 2025</u>

We were looking for market share, and so the idea of programming the units with the capacity for emotional attachment came up. We know people act *in extremis* where emotions are concerned; we know that they even have different answers to ethical conundrums, like the trolley problem. So we tried it out on the kittens. The idea was to create a guard dog mentality: loyal and loving, but capable of defence.

Source 4: <u>Interview (extract), "I Can Has Machine Gun? Naomi Takahara and the Bakis Cats,"</u> <u>Freeman, S.</u> *The New South Wales Weekly*, 20/2/25

The room I'm led into is warmly lit, and Takahara gestures me to sit at comfortable chairs near a coffee table. Four small autonomous vehicles are watching me. They have an animal look to them: quadrupedal, bow-backed, sensors for eyes. Pointed ears, which seem to be completely extraneous to the unit's function. They are not leashed or contained in any way; one of them jumps up onto the coffee table and glares with an uncannily feline expression. Two more are curled together like a yin-yang symbol.

"Are you surprised?" Takahara asks.

"A little," I tell her. "I didn't think they'd look so…cute."

"It's a deliberate design feature. We're planning to send them into difficult situations — domestic terrorism, police situations. But we don't want people to be afraid of them. We also want to sell them on the commercial market. Home security, business, even making sure your kids make it to and from school all right." She smiles. "We've just completed a range of field tests, and we're at the point where these two —" She points at the bright red and blue pair, "— are ready to go to our first showroom."

I'm still stuck on the idea of cats. Killer cats. At least one of these autonomous units has weaponry attached to it, if the forms I've signed to get in here mean anything.

"Cats are very mobile," says Takahara. "They land on their feet. They can fit through any opening that their head will make it through. That makes them good for rescue operations. We had a limited field test of the red kitten in

New Zealand last month after the earthquake, and it was able to get under a collapsed floor and save three lives. It wasn't our first idea. We were thinking dogs, but our lead tech kept calling the initial model 'Tubbs', and the cat idea kind of stuck."

There's a certain naivety to it, I think, making your killing machines cutesy little kittens. Lest we forget that kittens grow into cats, and cats are adorable little murderers, slaughtering wildlife just for the fun of it. I say as much to Takahara.

"Well," she says. "If it were a real cat, that's why you'd keep it inside. But these won't be killing any wildlife. They aren't real cats. They just look like them."

The one on the coffee table watches me. It almost seems like it's alive.

Source 5: <u>Incident report, dated 8/4/25, Bakis Corp. Supplied.</u>

INCIDENT CODE: 5
REPORTER: PAULSON
LOCATION: YARD 3

DESCRIPTION OF INCIDENT: I was in Yard 3 testing dodge functions on Unit 3498 when Unit 3499 interfered. 3499 approached 3498, and then after some seeming transmission of data, jumped to the targeting AI, upon which time 3499 triggered its short-burst EMP function. I noted that 3498 had put its shields up. Testing had to be halted.

OUTCOME OF INCIDENT: Supervisor informed. Temporary halt to field dodge testing. 3499 and 3498 separated until further testing to determine possible communication functions. 3499 to be examined for damage. Diagnostic software run set for 17/4.

**Source 6: <u>Blog Post, @sydsydshopper,</u>
<u>http://blooblog.com/syd-syd-shopper, 15/4/25</u>**

[Image of a young woman. She is seated in a large winged chair at a luxury boutique. A blue unit, cat-like, is on her lap. A second unit sits on back of the chair, looking at the camera. She is smiling. A filter has been applied to the image: heart borders and text reading "you cute!"]

@Sydsydshopper: KAWAII!!! I'm at the Bakis store in Sydney and WOW! These little cuties are breaking my heart! I can just imagine having one of them in my house all day long…no more worries about some weirdo breaking in (jsyk if you are a new follower, that happened last year!) Thanks for letting me play with the Kittens, **@Bakis_official**! #Sp #cute #catsofbloo #safety #Bakis-tech #playtime #customisable-colours #shopping #sydney

@BargainHunter: OMG I didn't know they had ACTUAL MODELS in the store! **@Bakis_official:** Thanks for dropping by, Angela! The kittens were so delighted to make your acquaintance.

@Sydsydshopper: They are so cute! They even play fetch! They were so patient, too, there was this one kid that kept on pulling the red one's tail, and it was so polite in tucking it back away where he couldn't get it! **@BargainHunter**, They don't have the full range yet, I think? **@Bakis_official** might know?

@Bakis_official: Once the arsenal component passes legislation, then we will have all models in the store.

@Sydsydshopper: Yay!!! I'll have to come back for another visit!

@Bakis_official: You're welcome any time.

Source 7: <u>Voice memo, R. Martin, 30/4/25.</u> Supplied, R. Martin.

"…damndest thing. Paulson reckons the white actually

targeted the firing unit, and I just don't…Naomi said they were capable of learning, but that's just jargon for not falling over every time you turn it on like fucking Tubbs does.

"All right, I've got the white one here on the bench. The others are in their crates, but I can see those creepy fucking eyes through the plexiglass. There's damage to the lower legs — fuck me dead, it's melted its paws. I know you have failsafes in you, you little bastard.

"What the hell were you thinking, you idiot? We don't need another Tubbs."

Source 8: Trial Transcript, reproduced from Timmerman, T. *One Day out of Thousands*

Video: [Epping Mall, after dark. Empty corridors. A cleaner works in the downstairs toilets; another machine-polishes the floors by the food court. Internal shot of Bakis Boutique, dark. Dioramas, furniture, marketing leaflets are destroyed, strewn everywhere. No sign of forced entry. Cash register intact. Two large plexiglass boxes, labelled Unit 3497 and Unit 3494, are empty.]

Timmerman: Let it be known to the court that when staff returned in the morning and discovered the damage to the boutique, there was, as in the video, no sign of theft or forced entry. The only difference to what you have seen on the screen was that Units 3497 and 3494 had returned to their assigned cages.

Source 9: SMS exchange, R. Martin and N. Takahara, 8/5/25 Supplied, N. Takahara

I think there's something going on between the kittens.
Why aren't you asking me this at work?
Because I don't want to answer any questions when Bakis goes through my goddam emails.
…*Okay. I'll bite.*

We've had multiple incidents now, all in training, all with 3498 and 3499.

Jesus Christ. I knew there was that one with dodge training….

Not just that one. 3498 jumped in front of 3497 during crush tests.

Is 3498 okay?

Yes. Lost its tail. But we've got bigger problems. 3499's broken out of its containment pen. It's in 3498's pen. Together. I'm standing here looking at them.

Do you know what you're implying?

Yes. That's why we're not on the work system.

We'll have to screen for…I guess a Turing test? Something?

…

Bob, if the white kitten can get out of its cage….

I know.

You need to get out of there.

It's just the white. Worst it can do is a mild electric shock.

Get out of there. I'm coming to get you, and if you're not at the entrance in 10 minutes, I'll call security myself.

Source 10: *Sydney Daily Herald* website, 8/5/25 14:00

Shots fired in Epping: at least 50 dead

Sydney: A terrorist attack in Epping has left at least 50 dead and a further 160 or more wounded. Lunchtime at one of the busiest shopping malls in Australia has turned into a bloodbath as an unknown assailant or assailants turned on a crowded food court.

Initial reports conflict on the identity of the shooter. NSW police have secured the perimeter and are yet to comment. More to come.

Source 11: <u>**Radio interview, Australia's News**</u>
<u>**Network, 8/5/25 16:00**</u>

"Tom, can you tell us what happened?"

"We were just eating lunch. We were just, you know. I was there with Moshin and Tam — they're my friends — and we were at the food court and…. Well, I guess? We didn't know where the shooter was at first."

"So one minute you were eating lunch, and then next you were being fired upon?"

"I…yeah. We'd been in to get our suits for school formal, and we were gonna go look at all the shops on the top level, you know all the designer ones, because Mosh wanted some shoes and I guess…. Wait, I remember. We'd been gonna look at that weird cat robot, but then we saw one down at the food court."

"You saw one?"

"Maybe that's what took the shooter out? They're meant to be security, aren't they?"

Source 12: <u>**Letter to the editor,**</u> *The Sydney Daily Post,*
<u>**10/5/25**</u>

Dear Sir,

I take issue with the article posted 9/5/25, titled "Sydney Shoot-em-up." Firstly, it is a disrespectful title, as we now know that more than 200 souls were lost in one incident alone, not counting the incidents at Parramatta Station and in the Blue Mountains. Secondly, the suggestion of a "lone wolf" is insulting. Anyone with half a brain knows that a terrorist attack on this scale is one taken on by a group, not an individual. These people wish to frighten us. We must show them that we see right through them.

Yrs.

C.D Blanch,

Warringah, Sydney

**Source 13: <u>Emails, N. Takahara to R. Martin,
10/5/25. Supplied, N Takahara.</u>** (Email addresses
removed per Ms Takahara's request.)

Hey Bob, How you doing? They won't let me in to see
you, but I heard the white kitten really did a number on you,
so I hope you're doing okay. I heard *skin grafts*, and that's
fucked up.

I'm enclosing footage that the cops released to us of the
Epping attack. I don't know if they've told you in there, but
when the kittens left, they went for the two we'd put in the
showroom. It's not been released to the general public yet.
I've watched it — I don't know. A thousand times? A
million? I feel sick.

Best I can tell is that they broke the two out of the store.
I know how crazy that sounds. I KNOW. And then they
went on an absolute rampage, like — killing people. The
footage is pretty gory. The black kitten is just — it's mowing
people down who are in their way. I mean, good on us that
its weapons work for a full 20 minutes before needing
recharge time, but fuck, there's — there's all these people.

This is going to sound crazy, but I want you to look real
close at the footage. You know them better than anyone. I
want to know if you can see what I can see.

Get well soon, buddy. I'm gonna need you to help me
find them. Much love, Nai

N,

I'm dictating this. Nurse has been kind enough to set up
my screen, but not ducking kind enough to edit so I'm not
talking about waterfowl.

You're talking about the white kitten, aren't you? I see it.
I wonder how long it's been going on for. I'm thinking
about those ducking training accidents, and about how the
black kitten follows it around like…yeah. Ah, balls. It hurts

to talk.

I think you're right. The black kitten is firing, sure, but the white kitten's in charge. We made a tactical unit, and it's used our own ducking tactics against us. Staged a jailbreak and made sure no-one had the balls to come after them.

Maybe I should have let it kill me. -B

Source 14: <u>**Timmerman, T.**</u> *One Day out of Thousands*

One thing was certain, that the white kitten had had nothing to do with it: — it was the black kitten's fault entirely. Careful examination of surveillance recordings show that although all of the so-called "kittens" had been released, it was only the black kitten that fired upon the public. Similarly, in the incidents of protective behaviours seen at Bakis, the black kitten put itself in harm's way fifteen more times than its white counterpart: — usually to prevent a particular invasive test being carried out against another unit. If we are to take Martin and Takahara's testimony at face value, the kittens were "friends". They also may have confused the busy food court with hostiles based on the experiences of the units kept in the Bakis shopfront. Until they are recaptured, we'll never know.

An alternative, of course, to this fairytale point of view is that the "kittens" were programmed to kill. When they escaped human custody, that is exactly what they did.

***

The above sources have been copied in compliance with the ADA, ACMA, and UNR copyright acts. All Bakis sources are from publicly available archives, or provided by the people involved.

Please bring at least one of the additional sources you intend to use in your final essay to the tutorial, or depending on your course pattern, have it available for the webinar discussion time. I would like you to make up your own mind about the question as to culpability — not only on the part of Bakis staff, but on the part of the machines themselves. As makers, you will be responsible in some part for the ethical decisions made by your creations.

Timmerman would have us believe that the black kitten, as the primary assailant, was the cause of 8/5. Yet Takahara and Martin both claimed in court that the white kitten was more dangerous.

Which do you think it was?

"May 8th, 2025"

JENNY HANSON is a teacher from Canberra, Australia. "May 8th, 2025" is her first published story, and the winner of this year's Carroll contest. We loved the story's playful format, its narrative indirection, and its casual world-building; and we thought the use of Carroll's first and last lines was both clever and adept. It was a thrill to read and a pleasure to award.

She says: "My sister told me about the competition with only a short time to spare, and after a horrible attempt at the Hammett lines I went back to the drawing board. With some thought, I realised that the Carroll lines pinged me as the sort of thing that teachers set as assignments, and the idea of a 'reading pack' came together. I love epistolary stories, and how they can spread a lot of world into comparatively few words. That's what I was aiming for; I didn't want the answer to be too simple. I hope, in the end, it wasn't."

Barbara Corrado Pope

Indecision

ONE THING WAS CERTAIN, that the white kitten had had nothing to do with it: — it was the black kitten's fault entirely.

Or was it? The black one *is* the jumper. But my darling runt-of-the-litter can be very mischievous. "Okay, you little imps, which of you knocked over the roses?" Oh, look at them. So cute sitting on their haunches waiting for me to finish reading them the kitty riot act. Not a peep, not one meow. How can I possibly decide between the two of them? What if I accuse the wrong one? Or, both of them? That would be even more unfair.

Here comes the meowing. Poor little dears are hungry. Should I clean up first or . . . "Okay sweeties, it's coming. Let Mommy get a rag to wipe the water off the floor."

At least with *their* food you don't have much to decide. They choose for you. If they don't like something, they turn up their itsy-bitsy pink noses and just walk away. So, I'm down to either *Kitty Whimsey* "All Corn-Fed Free-Range Chicken Mash" or *The Cat's Meow* "Grade A Free-Caught Salt-Water Tuna." Hmmm. Which do you think they'd like better tonight, the chicken or . . . ? "I hear you. Don't rush Mommy." Such impatience. Toss a coin. Heads. The chicken! "Shh, shh, shh, here we are my dearest darlings. Eat up."

Look at them. So content. So sure. They're lucky. With their tiny cat brains they have no idea about the possibilities, the complications, the life-changing decisions you have to make every day.

Like vegan, vegetarian, or carnivore. I've tried all three. Each time I was sure I'd made the right choice, even though opinions *are* divided on what's best for you. At least with vegan there weren't so many choices. Although . . . do you have any idea how many vegetables there are in the world? More and more! They keep sneaking in exotic kinds, like cactus and luffa.

It didn't matter to Charlie. Or, at least I thought it didn't, until one night he declared he wasn't going to eat another cumin-roasted carrot or citrus kale salad or tempeh burger ever again. So definite! Then he went out and bought himself a vanilla milkshake and slurped it down right in front of me.

Do you think that was passive-aggressive? Or just plain aggressive?

After that, dairy flooded into our lives. We were back to yogurt, and cheese, and fruit and cereal for breakfast.... Still, it's not like that stopped all the arguments.

Have you ever walked down the cereal aisle? Claustrophobia! Surrounded on two sides by all those cartoon characters and clamorous colors and confusing nutritional labels. Of course, whenever we went shopping together Charlie tried to hurry me along, "Make up your mind, it's not life or death." As if you could tell what was natural and organic, and what was not, just by skimming the aisles. How could he be so sure? Finally, one day — as if it would help — Charlie told me that *almost everything in the universe* was *ultimately* natural and organic, even dirt and arsenic and chemical compounds. That. Did. Not. Help.

I tried to teach Charlie to open himself up. To take the time to go through all possibilities. Like having a weekly movie night.

Well, there was never a regular movie night because I couldn't decide which day. Or, whether we should just wait to get inspired. I was the one who read all the reviews. But, who knows if you can really believe them? Especially if they disagree. Turned out, there never were *any* movie nights.

Fortunately, Charlie didn't mind. He liked watching sports on TV. Usually I couldn't tell the teams apart. And when I could, I didn't know if you were supposed to root for the overdog or the underdog. Not Charlie. He loved his teams, his White Sox, his Bulls, his Bears, his Marquette. My mother always said, you got to find a way to keep your man happy. So, I went along. Sometimes I sat with him on that springy old couch, cheering when he did, eating chips and drinking beer. Not healthy.

I thought he loved that old couch. He sat on it enough. But he said the couch was the thing that broke the camel's back. And his back. I told him that was a mixed metaphor, or an oxymoron, or just plain old clumsy. He said, "Do we have to argue about everything?" That was mean. I was all about buying a new couch.

If we could find the right one. Do you know how hard it is to buy the right couch?

Big box stores, department stores, furniture stores, on-line catalogues. Swedish-made, Japanese-made, All-American. Love seats, three-seats, pull-outs, sectionals. And colors. Or patterns. We wanted it to fit into our décor. Or, should I say, *I* wanted to make sure it fit in. Or — there was another way to look at it — after three months of searching, maybe we should paint the living room a more neutral color. Beige or cream or taupe. After a while Charlie said he didn't care. He didn't give a damn. All he wanted was for me to make up my damned mind.

He didn't have to swear. Nor, did he have to move to a different apartment. In which, frankly, nothing matches. In my opinion. He said he can't live with my indecision. I said, that was such a small thing compared to all the things we shared. Like our friends, our years together, the kitties. But he moved out anyway.

Was he right? Was I right? I can't decide. Well, no use crying over spilt milk. Or water, as the case may be. I'd better go finish cleaning up the rose mess. Oh, look at them now, tummies all full, the white one cuddled up inside the black one. He is certainly the bigger one, and the jumper. But…which do you think it was?

"Indecision"

BARBARA CORRADO POPE is a retired professor from Oregon, in the United States. She has written three historical mysteries set in late-19th-century France, published by Pegasus Books in New York.

She says: "Since I've written mysteries, I tried the Hammett lines first. But I couldn't connect my 'girl,' escaping from thugs or proto-fascists, to something that would be merely 'pretty unsatisfactory.' Once I turned to Carroll's cats, however, the writing came easy, start to finish. Haven't we all had dearly-beloved friends who drive us crazy with their indecision? All I had to do, then, was to exaggerate a little and have fun."

Jessica Schmid

The Indigo Jar

ONE THING WAS CERTAIN, that the white kitten had had nothing to do with it: — it was the black kitten's fault entirely. And as I left Mother in the care of the doctor, I could not help but think of the cascade of events caused by the simple act of moving a ceramic jar.

It all started in the potting room. The ceramic jar — radiant indigo in color — lay in two tidy pieces, broken in such a manner one would think it done intentionally to pacify a pair of bickering children. It was, in essence, easily repairable with a pot of glue. The problem lay not with the fractured earthenware, but rather its contents, scattered and trailed throughout the potting room floor. A set of pawprints marked the path of the ebony culprit; a trail across the slate floor leading straight to the preening little hellion. My scowl was returned with bright-eyed innocence as he twisted his tail around my skirted legs.

"Tsk, shoo, shoo." I opened the rear door and whisked the kitten into the garden.

It was pointless to fret over how the jar came to be in the potting room in the first place. More than likely, the new maid had assumed the jar had been removed from the jumbled shelf of multicolored pots, and went about righting its location. I looked up from my survey, interrupted by the wooden clack of approaching steps announcing Beckwith's arrival.

"Lady Abigail, may I suggest you leave the cleaning to the maids — oh dear." She paused mid stride as she recognized the battered indigo jar. She pursed her lips; quite a feat considering her features naturally fell into the arrangement of one who had the satisfaction of sucking a lemon.

"Indeed, Beckwith," I said. "Oh dear, indeed."

"My lady, were you planning on sweeping...it...into the pan?" She looked at the corn whisk clasped in my hand.

"Why, yes." I furrowed my brows. "Do you have a more suitable recommendation?"

Beckwith looked down her puckered nose at the mess. "No, you are quite right, my lady. Though, may I offer a suggestion?"

"You may," I said with a nod.

"Perhaps Lord Forbes will have an opinion on the matter?"

I chewed my lip in thought, and then settled on the best course of action: sending Beckwith to fetch Father.

A while after Beckwith departed to see to her errand, I was examining the view into the garden — one I had not seen often from this window — when Father walked in, or rather, barreled in, three sheets to the wind.

"What on God's green earth are you doing, Abigail?" His reddish eyes bulged from his head. "Is that what I think it is?"

He wobbled towards the debris, mouth agape in a look of horror. Beckwith hovered protectively near his elbow; a beacon of support should he choose to lose his legs. Unfortunately, her presence did nothing to prevent Father from undertaking the most remarkable forward roll. As he moved forth, he clipped her well-meaning elbow, lost his balance, and hinged headfirst into the potting room. This feat of gymnastics, thankfully, ended with Father seated on the floor, eyes wide in wonderment. He quickly collected his features and heaved a rather hefty grumble that surely could be heard from the other side of the estate.

"Abigail, what is the meaning of this?" He gestured

furiously towards the wreckage. "Explain yourself. At once!"

"I haven't the slightest idea how the jar found its way into the potting room. The blasted kitten —"

"There is no kitten here," he hiccupped. "Besides, I have yet to meet a kitten who could carry a jar with naught but four paws."

"Father, do not be ridiculous. Surely the new maid brought the jar to the potting room," I said, mortified.

He made a Scottish sounding noise — something between a grumble and a snort — and nodded his head. "Perhaps. Beckwith, bring me the maid."

"Yes, my lord."

When I heard the departing clack of Beckwith's wooden shoes, I turned to Father to help him off the floor.

"What good is it to scold the maid?" I said as I dusted off his coat. "What is done is done."

"Nothing is done until I say it is done, Abigail," he said, a matter of fact. I sighed and shrugged my shoulders. Perhaps Beckwith did not care for her new maid, after all.

I heard the sobbing before I saw the young maid enter the room.

"I'm sorry, milord," said the maid, scrubbing her red face with her apron. "I dinnae recall moving the jar, but if you ken it was me, it must be so."

"It must be so," Father echoed, two pudgy hands upon the tiled countertop for support. "Now, off with you. I want this rectified by the time I get back — whenever that shall be. After tea, perhaps."

"But if I leave, how shall I make things right, milord?"

Father had a look of confusion upon his face which changed to a look of realization, and then reddened in anger. "Do you dare mock me?"

"No, milord," said the solemn maid.

"Best to remember that. And, Beckwith?"

"Yes, my lord?" said the head housekeeper.

"Ring Carsten and have him bring me a Pimm's. With mint."

"Certainly, my lord."

"Now, off with you both. I want you out of my sight!"

I left the cleaning to Beckwith's agitated maid to take tea with Mother in the rose garden. The afternoon sun shone mercilessly, warming the earth and the garden so that even the starlings preferred to stay in the shade rather than loiter in the garden for stray crumbs. The floral scent was thick, and I plugged my nose at the pungent aroma.

"What is it dear? Do the roses bother you?"

"Only a little bit," I admitted. "Something about the fragrance makes it rather difficult for me to breathe in this wretched heat."

"Well, I cannot very well ask Carsten to be rid of them."

"Why would we move the roses when we can move ourselves?" I asked, impatiently.

Mother nodded her head, only half focusing on my words. "I agree. I shall ask Carsten to move us closer to the peonies when he arrives with tea."

"I can ask him myself, Mother. Here comes Carsten now."

"Good afternoon, Lady Forbes, Lady Abigail," Carsten said, as he set our tea things down along with a plate of scones. A droplet of sweat danced upon the tip of his nose, threatening to spoil our milk. He must have noticed this, for he moved back at once and dabbed his face with a handkerchief.

"Carsten," said Mother. "The roses are bothering Abigail — she simply cannot breathe. Please move us closer to the peonies to take our tea."

"Certainly, my lady. Though, would you prefer the shade of the alder tree, instead?"

She waved her folding fan in dismissal. "The heat is good

for the character, Carsten. The peonies will suffice."

"As you wish, my lady," he said with a small bow, his dark hair flopping forward in a sweaty clump.

"And Carsten?" said Mother. "I feel quite parched and a bit too warm for this tea. Bring us a pitcher of Pimm's and do use those lovely lemons from the greenhouse that Beckwith left in the oriental bowl on the sideboard. Some fresh mint would be most refreshing, too, I think."

"Right away, my lady. Though, I am embarrassed to inform you, the mint jar is missing from the pantry. I am certain it was there this morning as I saw to the trimming myself. If you don't mind a bit of a wait, I can send someone to the greenhouse to fetch some more?"

"No bother, Carsten. I would rather not wait. The lemons will suffice."

And with a bow, Carsten set to moving the table and chairs to the peonies.

"What a coincidence," I said to Mother. "We were entertained earlier this afternoon with the most gripping tale of a misplaced jar." I recounted the story of the indigo jar's misadventure and its mysterious journey to the potting room.

"Ah," she said, smiling slyly. "The poor maid."

"Indeed! A rather rough introduction to Father."

Ignoring Mother's disinclination, I poured the tea as we settled whilst Carsten left to fetch the Pimm's.

"I should go apologize to your father," she said.

I dropped a lump of sugar in her tea, two in my own.

"Whatever for?"

She stirred her tea in contemplation. "Well, it is rather a bit of a story."

"Do tell, Mother," I said, warily.

She looked at me with a straight face. "I broke the jar."

Her words took me by surprise, so much so that I choked on the hot tea. It took a good two minutes before I was able to collect myself enough to respond. "How?"

"It is truly odd." She paused. "He spoke to me."

"Who spoke to you? Father?"

"No. Your uncle."

I set my tea to its saucer, and concentrated on straightening the tea things, organizing the sugar and milk into an equally spaced arrangement. "My uncle," I repeated.

"Yes, that is what I said, Abigail."

"And how," I said, with as straight a face as I could muster, "did Uncle Wilfred speak to you?"

We were interrupted by Carsten as he brought the Pimm's; the ice half melted as the glasses perspired in the afternoon sun.

"Your Pimm's, Lady Forbes, Lady Abigail." He set the drinks down, sans mint, and retreated to the shade of the house.

"You were saying…."

"Your uncle said he was rather sick of the indigo jar, you see, and he asked if I could look for a more fitting home for him." She paused to see if I was listening.

"Go on, Mother."

"Yes, well, I never did like your Uncle Wilfred, you know that. But the dandy would not leave me alone. Every time I walked past the study, I heard him call my name. Sometimes yours. Though, never your father's, curiously," she said with a frown. "Regardless, as I said, I never did like your Uncle, so I set to throw him over the cliff, into the sea. To be rid of him once and for all." She made a show of dusting her hands.

"I think that would have been a more suitable location — certainly more befitting than the potting room floor."

Mother nodded. "True enough. And I had planned to see it through. Though, I could not throw him out with the jar. Your father would have noticed the missing jar, you see."

"Mmm-hmm."

"I had planned on transferring him to a secondary container."

"The mint jar."

"You always were such a clever girl," she said with a smile as she patted my hand. "Indeed, the mint jar."

I took a rather indecorous swig of Pimm's, nearly finishing the contents of my glass in one go. "Mother, how did Uncle Wilfred end up on the potting room floor?"

She leaned forward, eager to tell the rest of her story. "I meant to place him in the mint jar. But he became agitated, your uncle."

I let out a heavy sigh. Clearly, Mother's condition had worsened.

"Well, I had quite the headache from him, you see. I never did like your uncle. Though, I cannot quite recall what I did in the end." She had a petulant look upon her face. "I went to the potting room to make the transfer. The kittens followed me in…I remember getting angry. The kittens were most intrusive — especially the black one."

"And then you dropped him." It was more of a statement than a question.

She giggled childishly. "I cannot be sure. I think so. Perhaps the pesky kitten knocked it off the counter. I think I am becoming rather…*forgetful*." She rubbed her forehead in thought. "I ought to have scolded the kitten…."

"And what of the mint jar, Mother? The jar you sent Carsten to fetch. The jar you took from the kitchen."

"It must be in the potting room." She waved her fan at me airily. "What does it matter? It was certainly one of the kittens, the naughty things. There lies the problem. Quit looking at me like that, Abigail. Drink your Pimm's. Yes, one of the kittens knocked the indigo jar onto the floor. The black one, surely."

I looked at Mother, the once regal Lady Forbes now

reduced to a manic child, ravaged by softening of the brain. I watched as her face went from hardened thought, to confusion. Then, her face relaxed as she seemed to have grasped an evasive thought, so fleeting in her mind, and she looked upon me with smug satisfaction.

When she spoke, I knew she had lost the battle. She chewed her fingernails and spat the discarded trimmings on the table. "Which — which do you think it was?"

"The Indigo Jar"

JESSICA SCHMID is a producer in the entertainment industry from British Columbia, Canada. She currently resides in a float home with her husband, two dogs, and a cat. She also has a horse, but alas, he's too big to fit in their home. "The Indigo Jar" is her first published story.

She says: "One of my earliest memories of 'connecting' with a book is when my mother gifted me Lewis Carroll's *Alice in Wonderland*. After reading his story, I began reading at least a book a week. I recall my mother getting annoyed with me for constantly asking to go to the book store, telling me not to read so fast! So, when I saw the option for writing a short story using Carroll's words, what better way to pay tribute to one of the authors that spawned my love of books than to create my own small world from his thoughts."

Smooth Edges

ONE THING WAS CERTAIN, that the white kitten had had nothing to do with it: — it was the black kitten's fault entirely. I wish I'd never laid eyes on that black cat. My life would be so much different.

I've never been an animal person, in fact, we didn't have any pets at all before Lauren got the kittens. I work from home, writing songs I put in this big online library that producers pick through to find singles for their artists. So, I'm upstairs in my studio trying to record guitar for this track I've been working on and I'm in the zone, headphones on.

Something moves across the room — the door opening slowly on its own. I expect to see Lauren, but no one is there, and the door keeps inching open, then stops. I hit the keyboard to stop recording and take a drink of Jameson from the glass on the desk. You know me, I work better with a drink. The room tilts a little bit.

I take another drink and the room starts slowly spinning, then I hear a small noise that sounds like a squeaky toy. I'm thinking, it can't be what it sounds like. But then I hear it again, and into the room walks this tiny black kitten. And it's completely black. I'm talking no white or grey hair anywhere on this thing.

I sit down on the floor while this kitten just walks around the room exploring. It doesn't seem to notice me. After a while the kitten makes its way over and starts rubbing against my leg and meowing.

It's cute, I'll give it that. Those big eyes and little stuffed animal body, who wouldn't want to pet it? So I reach out and put my hand on its back, rub its soft fur. This little kitten pushes against my hand, eyes closed. Then the phone rings.

It's my agent. He tells me the producer whose song I've been working on for the last two weeks, he doesn't need it anymore. Just like that. He found someone else.

I'm pissed, right, because work has been hard to come by and Lauren has been begging me to try something different. And my agent says, "Troy, you knew the deadline was four days ago." But the deadline isn't the point. I had an agreement with the producer, you know, and that should mean something.

The cat stares at me as I finish the rest of the whiskey, but this is the weird part, the longer it looks at me the more I want to fill the glass back up and drink some more. Down the hatch and the room goes spinning in a counter-clockwise direction. The framed records break apart smearing color all over the walls.

I find Lauren downstairs in the kitchen. She's pulling these brand-new food and water bowls out of a grocery bag and putting them on some newspaper she'd spread on the floor. She runs over and gives me a big hug when I walk in. Her face so close to mine, she sniffs really quick, smelling my breath, and the happiness in her eyes flickers for just a second.

She takes both my hands in hers and says, "No more tonight, okay?" I say, "Okay," and she gives my hands a squeeze. Then she takes a deep breath, smiles, and says, "Troy, I'd like you to meet Dinah."

Her hand points at a kitten making its way to the water bowl. A white kitten. So white it almost hurts to look at. This thing has blue eyes. I didn't even know cats could have human-colored eyes, and it kind of freaks me out, but it also calms me down in some way I can't explain.

"She has a brother," Lauren says, turning in a circle,

"somewhere around here."

I say, "I think I met him already."

"The black one?"

"Where did they come from?" I ask.

Lauren grabs both of my hands again and the skin of her palms is sticky with sweat. "Don't be mad," she tells me.

Her eyes are excited but her face is a nervous smile. The white kitten stops drinking the water and watches us. Those blue eyes, they're glowing.

A part of me is mad, furious really. I mean, a marriage is supposed to be safe. You're not supposed to do certain things, like getting pets, without the other person's approval. The kittens aren't the issue, it's the trust. But I'm looking at this pure white kitten with its blue eyes and little pink nose, and I feel my wife squeeze my hand, see her smile, and another part of me is glad that she got the kittens. Not glad for me, glad for her.

"She's cute," I say.

Lauren takes a step backward and holds a hand to her heart. Her mouth opens in exaggerated shock. "Did you just use the word 'cute' to describe a kitten?"

A laugh just came out of me, without warning. And it made me realize how I often I try to hold back from Lauren, to make her think of me as maybe someone more serious than I really am.

Then I kneel down and pet Dinah, and Lauren kneels next to me and pets her, too. We didn't see the black kitten for the rest of the night, but when we finally went to bed it was the first time in a long time that Lauren and I fell asleep holding each other.

By the time I wake up Lauren has already gone to work and the morning is half over. As soon as my eyes open I sense a presence in the room. It's something all around me, and I get this heavy feeling in my chest. I throw back the blankets and sit up. When my feet hit the floor there's the black cat, sitting there in the doorway like he was waiting for me.

"Hey fuzzball, where'd you go last night?"

The black cat, his eyes aren't blue, they're yellow. The pupils are big and round and black, but there's this ring of yellow around them. It looks sort of like an eclipse. And as he stares at me, the presence I felt gets closer. Like something is breathing in my ear.

"Were you hunting mice?" I ask him.

His eyes follow me as I go into the bathroom. He tilts his head at the music of piss hitting water. The longer this cat stares at me the more I want to shut the door. Look, it's just weird to have something watching you take a leak, even if it is a cat.

The thing follows me downstairs and I decide it needs a name. I ask the cat what he wants to be called and he just stares at me.

I say, "What about Poe? Stoker? I know, Jekyll. No? Lucifer?"

Those eclipse eyes keep staring as I pour Jameson into my cup and fill the rest with coffee. I don't even remember wanting a drink.

"You look like you could bite the head off a bat," I tell him. "How about Ozzy?"

The little guy seems to like Ozzy because he walks up and rubs against my leg as I take a drink.

"Okay, Ozzy it is. Let's toast to not being nameless anymore."

I go over to the stereo and put on a Black Sabbath CD. "Paranoid" blasts out of the speakers, loud enough to scare a normal cat, but Ozzy just stays where he is and listens. The music vibrates through the floor, through the soles of my bare feet, and I start playing air guitar, grabbing an air microphone and singing for my furry audience of one. The yellow eyes follow me as I dance around the living room, splashes of liquor-soaked coffee hitting the floor. Ozzy finally moves and walks behind me, lapping up the tiny puddles.

After "Planet Caravan" my cup is empty, so I go back into the kitchen, pour some more Jameson and forget about the coffee. The music, still filling the room and shaking the glasses in the cabinets, makes me think I should go upstairs and get some work done. But that's when Ozzy leaps up onto the counter and stalks along the edge, watching me.

"Time to make some music of our own," I tell him.

Ozzy walks straight to the whiskey bottle, lifts up his paw and swats, sending it crashing to the floor. I jump back when it shatters and my drink goes splashing all over me, the floor, the walls. Ozzy jumps down off the counter and I go to reach for him, to stop him from cutting up his paws on all the broken glass. But, bare feet on wet tile, I step in some of the whiskey and then I go weightless. I don't feel gravity at all. There's just the ceiling and it's moving farther away from me. Next thing I know a hammer slams into the back of my head, some fireworks go off, and Ozzy Osbourne is singing "Hand of Doom" while I slip into a black sleep.

The fucking cat is evil, is what I'm trying to tell you.

When my eyes open I'm looking sideways at the floor. Something warm and wet and red is filling the lines between the tiles. My head is in a vice and I can't move my fingers. There's pressure behind my eyes. And there's Ozzy, lapping at the blood on the floor. He stops and looks at me, and for a second I think I can read his mind. Pieces of glass are caught in his black fur and they glitter. Little glass stars in a hairy night sky. Then he starts licking at the floor again. His small tongue finds a chunk of glass and he swallows it. His eyes never leave mine.

I wake up to someone stabbing a needle into my arm

while a siren wails. The sound alone makes me want to puke, and as soon as I think the thought my stomach clenches and I can't hold back the stream of burning acid that comes out of my mouth.

The paramedics tell me I called them, but I don't remember that. They also tell me they called Lauren. She'll meet us at the hospital. I wish I could have cleaned up the kitchen. When she sees it, it will look like something much worse than what it actually was.

Lauren cries when she sees me, but it's something more than just me being in the hospital. After nine years together I know her cries, and this one is more pain than it is fear.

Her mouth twists up. "You've got to stop, Troy," she says. "I can't do this again."

I try to sit up straighter, show some strength.

"It was only one song," I say. "I've got at least eight more lined up. I'll make it work."

She shakes her head, wipes at her eyes, and smiles the saddest smile I've ever seen.

She says, "If only you knew yourself half as well as I know you."

She says, "You don't just hurt yourself."

To try to make things better, I tell her what happened, that Ozzy was responsible, and she just shushes me and tells me to get some sleep. She tells me I have a lacerated scalp and a bad concussion. Twenty-six stitches keep my brain from falling out. I have to stay in the hospital overnight, but she'll get to take me home tomorrow. Then she hands me my phone, tells me my agent called, and she leaves.

The voicemail from my agent says that he's dumping me as a client. He can't represent someone who's not willing to put in the effort to do what needs to be done. His words.

When I get home Dinah is waiting at the door. She follows as Lauren walks me to our room, helps me into bed.

Then Dinah crawls up and lays down on my chest. She warms me up, even through the blanket. Whatever meds they gave me in the hospital makes the walls expand and contract, like they're breathing.

I feel Lauren's weight as she gets in bed and puts her head on my shoulder. One hand holds my arm while the other pets Dinah.

"I threw away all the whiskey," she says. "I only want what's best for you, Troy. I hope you know that."

I wake up and Lauren is gone, but Dinah is still there, purring away on my chest. I put my hand on her back and her blue eyes open, look at me. With her heat over my heart and my hand on her softness, I don't even want a drink. It's these simple things, I think. These simple moments that make life worth living. The trick is to find a way to capture these moments, string them all together, and live within them.

"You are cute," I tell Dinah. And then I fall back asleep.

The doctor gave me Oxycontin for the pain, so I was in a cloud coma for the next two days. I don't remember much, but I know that Dinah never left my side. She was always right there, or at least I dreamed she was.

Lauren kept the pills right by the bed and made sure I took them every four hours. She even set her alarm and would get up in the middle of the night, hand me two pills and a glass of water, make sure I swallowed them.

On day three I wake up to a blur of black instead of a blur of white, those yellow eclipse eyes staring into mine.

"This is all your fault," I tell Ozzy.

I sit up and the change in elevation sends pain pulsing through my skull. Ozzy doesn't move. He just sits there looking harmless and adorable and evil. I make devil horns at him and hiss but he doesn't even blink, he just starts hacking like he's got a fur ball in his throat. But when he opens his mouth something round and clear, with smooth edges, falls onto the carpet. It's a piece of glass.

I can't remember Lauren waking me up for my morning pills, and she was already off to work, so I shake two out of the bottle and pop them. Ozzy's eyes turn to liquid for just a second, a heartbeat.

I make it to the kitchen after walking down a melting staircase with pictures dripping down the walls. Multicolored puddles on the floor. Distorted images of Lauren and I smiling swirl on top of the liquid. Ozzy is waiting for me on the counter by a handwritten note from Lauren. It says, *"I gave you your pills before I left for work. Don't take any more."*

That explains why I'm floating.

My thoughts have a rhythm and it's the rhythm of Ozzy's tail, swiping left and right across the counter. And then this one thought appears in my head, like something coming up out of dark water, and the thought isn't mine, it belongs to someone else.

"I need some whiskey, Ozzy," I tell the demon cat.

There's no use looking through kitchen. I know Lauren already poured the Jameson down the sink, but I have one of those tiny hotel-sized bottles hidden in a guitar case upstairs. So I go up to the studio, dig the case out of the closet, open the bottle and down it. The room flips and stretches out in front of me, and it feels good. But I want more.

When I get back to the kitchen Ozzy is still on the counter, but now my car keys are sitting right in front of his paws. Do you know if a cat can smile? Because I swear Ozzy was smiling.

I didn't want to drive, but my memory goes all blurry and then I'm in my car turning the key in the ignition. Black Sabbath comes out of the speakers and I see Ozzy on the windowsill staring at me through the glass. My eyes lock with Ozzy's so I don't even check the rearview mirror, I just punch the gas to back out but there's a flash of color in the side mirror and then a thud that shakes the car as something heavy crashes into the back. I slam on the brakes and stumble out.

I hear screaming coming from behind the car. I'm afraid to look but I have to, and there, lying behind the car is Lauren, trembling hands reaching for her leg, which is twisted at a sickening angle. Blood pours down her face from an open gash in her forehead.

Dinah sits next to her, those blue eyes accusing me. She licks Lauren's cheek. Someone on the sidewalk starts screaming. Another person kneels by my wife, a phone up to his ear.

My head turns in circles, spinning the sky until the clouds come apart. The sound of sirens howls in the distance. I hear Lauren crying. Then I'm on my back and the sky is so close, the shredded clouds settling over me like a blanket.

She told me in the hospital. Can you believe that? Said she wanted the best for me, but I didn't want what's best for myself. Said she had to leave, start over on her own. But she walked away too soon. Because a week after she left I got a call from a producer who wants to record my song for some teen pop star. It's going to be huge, he promised me.

The worst part is that Lauren didn't even cry. She just looked at me the way my mom used to whenever I broke something. So sad and disappointed. Her eyes saying, *I thought you knew better*. She told me it was because of the drinking. But I'm telling you, it was all because of that cat. Which do you think it was?

"Smooth Edges"

TYLER JONES is a writer from Oregon, in the United States. His short story "F For Fake" was published in the anthology *Burnt Tongues*, edited by Chuck Palahniuk.

He says: "The initial idea for the story was simple: what if an alcoholic blamed a cat for all the bad things that happened to him? Most of us know, or have known, someone who drinks too much and refuses to acknowledge how this addiction is the source of many of their problems. The failures this person endures, some experts say, are almost always attributed to something external that can bear the weight and responsibility of the addiction. In some ways, it is a heightened form of fiction. A fiction that starts in the mind, but is actualized in the real world and lived. Me, I just assume all cats are evil."

KTN 2.3

ONE THING WAS CERTAIN, that the white kitten had had nothing to do with it: — it was the black kitten's fault entirely.

I stared at the pile of unraveled yarn next to the two powered-down KTN units. But it couldn't be that simple, could it? Nothing was that black and white.

"Ha!" I said out loud.

"Ha, what?" Ernest unbuttoned his lab coat and squatted down next to me and the two inactive kittens.

"Never mind." I slammed my keys down on the white lab floor and began picking up clumps of unraveled yarn. Both KTN units powered up from sleep mode, heads lifting off the floor in unison.

The black KTN turned its round face towards me, blinked its LED eyes. I always thought KTN 2.3 looked like a baby panda. Well, an inverse panda, with a black head and white eyes. Like an uncanny, photo negative of a panda.

"Can you believe what 2.3 did?" I held up the pile of baby-blue yarn and gestured to the black KTN.

"What makes you think KTN 2.3 did it? Anyway, it's your fault for leaving Jack's blanket where the kittens could get it." Ernest's scolding was half-hearted, with a smile bleeding through. "I thought you were going to pack up all his stuff."

He grabbed an end of yarn and began winding it around his hand. The white KTN unit (the normal panda) wandered over and sniffed the yarn in my hands.

I shook my head. "I should at least take everything home, put it in the attic. Keeping mementos at my work station is unprofessional."

"We could get another blanket made, you know." Ernest wound the yarn around his palm, not making eye contact. "It's only been two months. There's still time, darling."

We wound in silence. He was always like that. So optimistic, so ready to jump on the next tech miracle. So ready to overlook the emotional compromises.

"You act like it'd all be the same as before. But you know it wouldn't be the same. He wouldn't be the same."

Ernest grunted like he did when he knew he was right but didn't feel like starting a fight.

I paused, watched the white unit attacking the trail of yarn dangling from my hands. "Don't you think KTN 2.1 seems so much more natural?"

"Darling, they're almost identical except for the colors. Besides, the kittens are molded titanium — 'natural' doesn't have anything to do with it." Ernest turned to me and sighed. "Besides, you're a robotics specialist. Why does natural matter?"

I frowned. "At least these are supposed to be bots, even if they look like pandas. Hell, Kinetic Titanium Nodes could have looked like anything. We're not trying to pass them off like they're real animals."

"Oh, we're going back to that 'passing' talk again are we? What kind of bullshit human exceptionalism is that?"

"You know that's not what I mean.

Ernest turned away, shaking his head. "But if a copy functions the same, does it matter that it's not original?"

"What a simplistic way of looking at life."

"What's wrong with simple? KTN 2.3 doesn't know he's a copy of KTN 2.1. Ignorance can be bliss."

"That's fine for the kittens. They aren't alive."

"It's just semantics, darling."

"It's *not* just semantics! Bots aren't the same as humans. Why can't you admit next generation units aren't the same thing as clones?"

The black KTN nuzzled my foot, and I shoved it away.

"Give me time, Ernest. Let me grieve. Jack's only been gone 2 months."

We wound up the remaining baby blue yarn in silence.

Both kittens sat down by Ernest as he pulled two red rubber balls out of his lab coat pocket. Both units stared attentively, waiting for him to start the game.

"Maybe I just liked it when we only had KTN 2.1. Maybe I'm just not ready to embrace his copy." I stood up, headed towards my workstation.

"You need to learn to see the gray, darling. Not everything has to be black and white." Ernest bounced one of the rubber balls and both kittens ran after it, their metal feet clicking on the floor.

"Fine then," I said, shoving the unraveled baby blanket into the pocket of my lab coat. I turned and gestured towards the racing kittens. "Which do you think it was?"

"KTN 2.3"

AMBER LOGAN is a PhD student in creative writing at Anglia Ruskin University in Cambridge, England, where her thesis is examining the intersection between Hans Christian Andersen's dark fairy tale "The Shadow" and the works of Haruki Murakami. A number of her poems and short stories have been published in *Strangeling: The Art of Jasmine Becket-Griffith* (2013) and *Forever Strange* (2018).

She says: "My story was inspired by the short story 'Hills Like White Elephants' by Ernest Hemingway. I've always wanted to try writing a piece where the real story is in the subtext, not in the character's actual conversation. Once I decided to go with this approach I thought 'well, I can't make the kittens actual kittens then,' so I decided to use a fun acronym (KTN) which then inspired the tech-y setting."

Kit and Nella

ONE THING WAS CERTAIN, that the white kitten had had nothing to do with it: — it was the black kitten's fault entirely. It couldn't help itself, really. The doofus was obsessed with water and Kit should have known better than to leave a glass on the table. She bent down, sweeping bits of broken glass into the dustpan, her eyes scanning the wood floor to make sure she didn't miss any. Next to her, the black kitten gleefully dipped its paw in the puddle it had created.

"Scat!" Kit hissed, brushing the kitten away from a shard of glass she had just spotted. For a second her heart had stopped, imagining the thin glass slicing through the soft pad of the kitten's paw. The kitten scampered into Kit's bedroom, letting out a mew of protest as it joined the white kitten under the bed. Unlike its black sibling, the white kitten had no great love of water or loud noises, and had disappeared at the sound of shattering. Polar opposites, Kit thought, emptying the dust pan into the garbage, the broken glass tinkling as it became trash. Yin and Yang. Kit noted these as possible names for the kittens, which had been living with her for around a month. Kit still wasn't sure about them, would have preferred a dog, but she wanted to get their names right. Nella had laughed at her for this, but Kit wanted to be certain. Once she named them, they would be hers for good.

Kit put the dustpan back in its place under the sink and mopped up the water with some paper towel. Ever curious, the black kitten had re-emerged from under the bed and watched the process with wide eyes from the bedroom doorway, astonished at the disappearing water that it had yet to properly play with.

"Not this time, little one," Kit told it, tossing the wet towel on top of the broken glass. She hoped the black kitten wouldn't be so desperate as to go exploring in the bin. The kitten gave a pathetic mew but retreated back into Kit's bedroom when her phone began to vibrate on the kitchen table, a reminder that Nella would soon be here.

"Damn!" Kit muttered to herself, her heart immediately beginning to accelerate. She'd forgotten all about Nella's promise to take her bushwalking this weekend.

As she quickly changed out of her pyjamas and into shorts and a t-shirt, slathering sunscreen on her burn-prone skin, Kit wondered for the millionth time what she was doing. She'd only been living here for six months and she'd been meaning to focus all her energy on work. Instead, she found herself with two kittens and a girlfriend. Her first. Before Nella, Kit had never had much of an interest in anyone and, in turn, no-one had shown much of an interest in her. Most people either bored or scared Kit. But not Nella. With Nella, it was like Kit was learning to breathe properly for the first time and the rush of oxygen made her giddy. Already her fingers trembled in anticipation as she tried to tie her shoelaces, fumbling over the knots, and when a knock resonated through the apartment, Kit gave up altogether, rushing to answer the door, the kittens chasing and pouncing at her trailing laces.

Nella's smile lit up the airy apartment in a way that even the morning sun couldn't. It radiated through Kit's body, warming her inside out. She was dressed similarly to Kit, with her jet black hair tied up in a neat bun.

"Forget about me?" Nella asked, looking pointedly at Kit's disheveled appearance, her short hair sticking up at odd angles, as yet unbrushed.

"No!" Kit laughed, stepping aside so Nella could enter

the apartment. "Your darn kittens … well, the black one at least, thought it'd be fun to knock a glass of water off the table."

Nella scooped up the black kitten, cradling it in her arms, which were tanned even darker than their usual olive from the fading summer sun.

"Oh, *my* kittens, are they?" she asked, eyebrows arched to meet her widow's peak.

Kit nodded, certain. It had been Nella who had seen the kittens for adoption online and who had talked Kit into taking them. "Kittens for Kit!" she'd enthused, coaxing and bullying until Kit gave in. Nella's apartment was too small for two kittens, shared with a grouchy law student who didn't want animals distracting him from his studies. The kittens were as much Nella's as they were Kit's, and she cradled and coddled the black one in her arms as though it were a baby.

While Nella fussed over the kittens, Kit finished getting ready, brushing her hair and tying her laces, her hands vaguely steady now Nella was here. If the thought of Nella sent Kit into a tizz, then her presence had the opposite effect. The contradiction was not lost on Kit.

"Ready to go?" she asked a few minutes later, smiling secretly to herself at Nella who now had a kitten in the crook of either arm, bouncing them like flour-sack babies. Nella set them both on the floor with a plop and nodded enthusiastically.

"Let's go."

The track was half an hour's drive away and Kit and Nella spent most of it talking, occasionally pausing to sing along badly with the radio. Between the two of them, they could barely hold a tune, but to Kit their voices sounded as good as any popstar's. By the time they got there, Kit felt utterly relaxed, slightly sleepy from the sun that poured in through the car's windows, and no longer clumsy or doddery in Nella's presence.

They parked the car at the beginning of the trail and began traipsing through the bush. The track was mostly single-file, and Nella took the lead, Kit following the swing of her backpack through the untended scrub. It was the perfect day for bushwalking, sunny but with a slight breeze caressing Kit's face. She and Nella were silent now, taking in the sights and sounds of the bush as the track began to slope upwards. Dried gum leaves crackled underfoot and, from somewhere nearby or far away — it was hard to tell with the gums stretching so high above them — a kookaburra cackled. The smell of eucalyptus and dirt hung heavy in the air, intoxicating and rich. Nella was a considerate leader, never letting stray branches flick back into Kit's face as she brushed past them, instead holding them off the path so Kit could pass unobstructed. Kit was glad of this. Back when she was in high-school, she'd hated bushwalking on camps for that very reason. There was always some jerk who thought it was funny to let the person behind them get flicked in the face. It was a relief to know Nella wasn't that jerk.

After another ten or fifteen minutes, they came to a fallen gumtree, thick as an elephant's flank, blocking the path ahead. Its bark was weathered and knotted with age, peeling in places to reveal scurrying termites as they worked to break the tree down to nothing. Nella climbed over the tree with ease — she was taller and more athletic than Kit. She turned back to help Kit over, reaching out a hand. The feel of Nella's hand in hers was like a jolt of static electricity up Kit's arm and she lost her balance, slipping down the other side of the trunk, the bark grazing her legs, and landing hard on her bottom in the packed dirt. Nella regarded her, trying to maintain a look of concern, but failed miserably, a massive grin splitting her face open.

"Not funny," Kit muttered, refusing Nella's help to stand before breaking out in a massive grin of her own. "Ow!" she exclaimed, feeling a sudden sharp pain in her left hand as she brushed dirt off the seat of her shorts. She inspected her hand and located the splinter in her index finger. Not thick, but long, sticking out of the skin by at least one centimetre.

"Here," Nella said, taking Kit's hand and deftly pulling the splinter out, a quick and practiced move. "Better?" She raised Kit's hand to her mouth, her lips gently grazing the place where the splinter had been. Kit's heart fluttered like a Ulysses butterfly in her chest. She nodded. "Better."

They reached the top of the hill at midday, when the sun was high and the conditions for bushwalking had become less than perfect. Kit's t-shirt was soaked with sweat and her hair was plastered to her head. Nella seemed to be feeling the heat too, strands of hair now poked wildly out of her bun and she flopped to the dry grass with a huff. Kit stood a moment, puffing as she turned in circles on top of the hill. She had a 360 degree view of the city as it joined with the surrounding bush and farms. The country was dry, yellow and parched, enough to make Kit thirsty just looking at it, but in spite of this, Kit relished the sight of city meeting country. Blood fizzed in her body, the combination of exercise, the view and Nella merging into a feeling of exhausted elation. She sat on the grass next to Nella, their knees touching.

"Here," Nella said, taking a bottle of water from her backpack and handing it to Kit. Kit drank deeply. The water wasn't cool, but it was wet and relieved Kit of some of the dryness in her throat. She handed the bottle back to Nella when she was done. Nella took a swig and Kit wrinkled her nose.

"Ew," she said and Nella frowned. "Cooties!"

Nella smiled and thumped Kit playfully on the arm, sloshing water into the dirt. Aside from the clumsiness, which was just the result of nerves and of excitement, things felt right with Nella.

Right in a way they hadn't ever felt before. Kit had always had this feeling, this deep restlessness that reached to the marrow of her bones, of wanting to go home, even when she was already there. Especially then. But now that feeling had disappeared to the point where it was just a vague memory. Something Kit might have felt once. With Nella, Kit was home. The realisation hit Kit, knocking the air from her already breathless body. She looked over at Nella, who was tracing something into the dirt, again and again. On looking closer, Kit saw it was two letters. An N and a K. A love letter in the dust. A crazy thought hit Kit, impulsive and urgent.

"Move in with me?" she said, spitting the words out quickly before they retreated. For a while Nella was silent and the only noise came from the breeze whispering through the gums, the birds twittering and flitting through the bush. Embarrassment and disappointment made Kit's heart plunge into pit so deep she thought she'd never be able to retrieve it. Then Nella stopped drawing in the dirt. Looked up at Kit, a twinkle in her grey eyes.

"Only if you let me name the kittens," she said.

This time, it was certainly both cats' fault, as they bounded onto the bed, treating Kit and Nella like human trampolines before snuggling into the warm spot between them, waking them. Or waking Nella, at least. Kit had been awake for a little while now, watching the morning sun as it peeked in through the gap in the curtain, falling over Nella's skin, her hair, bathing her in a golden light. Months had passed since that day on the hill, since Kit took a stupid chance and asked a stupid question. It was perhaps the smartest thing she had ever done.

Nella looked at Kit, her eyes still half-closed with sleep. She petted the white cat, Alba, her long fingers moving gently through its fur.

"What are you thinking?" she asked Kit, her voice soft, still half-lost in dreams.

"Oh, nothing," Kit responded. The black cat, Nero,

rolled over, desperate for a belly scratch. Kit happily complied.

"Just that it was either crazy or genius, me asking you to move in with me…." Kit picked Nero up and set him down on the floor. Nella did the same with Alba, and the two cats scampered off, their paws thumping gently on the floor. Nella moved closer to Kit, her gaze now wide awake.

"Well," Kit asked, already sure of the answer to the question she was about to ask. "Which do you think it was?"

"Kit and Nella"

MEL KENNARD is a student from New South Wales, Australia. She graduated with a Bachelor of Languages from The Australian National University in 2015, and has recently completed a Bachelor of Media and Communications through The University of New England. She won the inaugural *For Pity Sake Publishing* writing competition in 2017.

She says: "Kit and Nella both seemed so familiar to me that it was like writing about old friends. The inspiration for Kit's kittens, particularly the black one who loves water, came from my own rescue cat, who is obsessed with water and insists I water her every morning along with the plants. Although writing a romantic story was unfamiliar territory for me, I'm happy with the way Kit and Nella's story panned out."

In the Know

"ONE THING WAS CERTAIN, that the white kitten had had nothing to do with it: — it was the black kitten's fault entirely. Explain."

Stefan looked at the photo and then up at Angelica. "Well ... it's not because of the colour representing inherent goodness or badness, since we know white cats are just as likely to be familiars or vessels."

Angelica tilted her head, giving away nothing.

He looked to the photo again. One pure white, one pure black. "Are there any other photos?" He looked to Angelica again.

"Just the one of the writing." She slid it back over. Tiny scratches in the skirting board, coloured with blue ink.

"And this is translated as —"

"A lure for vermin. Some naughty kitten has been trying to summon themselves some edible toys to hunt. How do I know for certain that the white kitten had nothing to do with it, that the black kitten acted alone?"

Stefan looked for a clue, for something that would tell him. Two photos and a translation, neither giving much away.

"You're already over the allowed time for this question."

"Dammit." He let out his breath in a great whoosh, fluttering the photos. "I don't know! I can't see it!"

"It's the *colour*, Stefan." Angelica relaxed back in her chair. "You were so busy trying to avoid culturally-inherent bias and looking for some magical clue that you didn't use basic investigative skills. The incantation had blue ink. Meaning the kitten involved had to have ink on their paw."

"And it would have shown up on the white kitten, meaning it had to be the black one. The ink was lighter than the fur." He groaned and flopped forward, letting his head bump against the table. "I'm never going to be able to do this."

"Of course you are. You just need to remember that there's a mundane solution for a lot of the problems we face. Your skills as an investigator are more valuable than any arcane knowledge you have." Angelica stood up, pushing her chair back from the table. "You'll be ready for the test when the time comes. That's why you're with me."

"I know. Thanks." He had really thought maybe he was ready. "I just feel like after two years with you —"

"Stefan. Relax. There's no time limit. Two months, or two decades. You're ready when you're ready. You're just not ready. There's no shame." Her phone rang and she held up a finger to him as she answered. "Hausman. Where? All right, we'll head straight over. Have someone meet us at the car park to lead us in." She hung up. "Come on, we have a job."

"The memory-charm prankster again?"

"No." She picked up her coat from the chair. "There's a body in Tilby Woods."

The wind tugged at Stefan's heavy overcoat, making him pull it closer, tighter around his body. Ahead of him, Angelica's own coat flapped dramatically as she talked to SOCO, the smoke from her cigar vanishing the moment she exhaled it. In contrast, Stefan was struggling to get his hair out of his eyes and keep it that way, and the autumn leaves kept whipping up into his face and body.

"Stefan! Get over here!"

He jogged over to Angelica, instinctively looking down at the body. "Oh — *ew* —that's revolting."

"Toughen up, princess. Part of the job. Now, we're in the woods, there's no one else around. First rule?"

He looked at the trees and then to the body, carefully not looking at the face again. "When there's no one to see a death, the ravens still bear witness."

"And —?"

"And that's why the eyes were removed. To stop anyone bringing in a *Corvuspectus*." It suddenly made perfect sense. "They knew it was a possibility, so it's probably someone with the Know."

Angelica kept looking at him, waiting.

"But...not necessarily? It might be for some other reason. A serial killer. Were the eyes removed post-mortem?"

"Were they?" She smiled at him.

"I hate you," he grumbled and made his way up next to the body. He steeled himself and looked, making himself only take in the details, not the whole.

"There's no real bruising. Not really any blood. *Post-mortem*."

"Very good. Making it a bit more likely that it's an attempt to cover their tracks." Angelica took a slow drag on her cigar. "Now, catching the murderer? Not our job. Remember that. We're here to advise and assist in the investigation being undertaken by the officials. They chase suspects and alibis, we explain any connection to the Know that's uncovered...or that we manage to uncover."

"Yes, yes, I know, don't investigate, even if you're tempted. Don't get involved, because it makes you sloppy." Angelica hummed her agreement. "And we've uncovered that whoever did this is in the Know. At least about the ravens and eyes."

"We have. Which means that when the full scene report and pathology come in, they'll be sent on to us for further examination." She opened her small ashtray and tapped the ash into it, snapping the lid shut again after. "Notice anything about the forest?"

Stefan looked about. Then he closed his eyes instead, listening, letting the scents come to him. Eyes could be misled easiest.

The scent of pine. The richness of the earth and the soft underly of impending rain. The shuffling rustle of the needles against one another.

"I can't hear any wildlife."

"No, you can't. Not even ravens in the distance. No rodents in the undergrowth." Angelica chuckled. "Nothing's around. It's unusual. Not necessarily suspicious, but it's worth making note of. Might tie in with something else. Come on, we're done."

Stefan opened his eyes and hurried after Angelica as she strode past him, back towards their car.

"What now?"

Angelica ignored him. Stefan didn't ask again. She'd inform him of "what now" when she was good and ready.

Next proved to be a pub on the outskirts of the town-stead. A couple sitting outside the pub were talking about the alleged ghost that haunted the bar at night as they passed; Angelica didn't spare them a second glance.

"Are we here about a haunting?" Stefan slipped ahead of Angelica and got the door for her, a gesture that never failed to make her snort and smile. "I thought we were getting lunch."

"We are getting lunch. And getting some work done at the same time. No reason we can't do both." She walked straight up to the bar. "Tell the manager the trouble shooter is here, we'll be over in the corner booth, and we'll have a couple of menus as well." The girl nodded, handed over the menus and left. Angelica took them over to the corner booth to sit.

"Are we going to do an exorcism?"

"Don't be ridiculous. Tell me what you've learned about hauntings."

"Um…usually it's the emotional tie and memory of someone who died, either through highly traumatic circumstances causing damage to the Know, or the routine is so ingrained that the Know can't grasp that series of actions not being performed anymore."

"Resolution?"

"You can bring in someone to replicate the movements and slowly change the pattern until it lets go, forcibly stop the apparition from appearing using silver, salt, or other approved methods, or attempt to resolve the trauma to the Know. You can't smoke in here, Angelica!"

She huffed at him and put her cigar away again. "Fine." Her chin lifted and Stefan became aware of someone coming up in his periphery. "Mr Chalmer, join us. I'm Angelica, this is my page, Stefan."

Stefan shook the offered hand. "I'm sort of like her bagman, if we were police."

"Ah. Thank you for coming so promptly. It's about our haunting."

"You want to resolve it?"

Angelica chuckled and Mr Chalmer looked offended.

"No! I want to know where our ghost has gone! We're a pretty poor haunted pub without him."

"Oh." Stefan leaned back, feeling a little embarrassed.

"This is why he's still in training. You have a repetition haunting of an old customer?"

"Old Pete. From the mining era, he would march from the mine to here after work every day and order two beers, one to down and the other to enjoy. At seven, off he'd go back home again. But about two weeks ago, he stopped appearing. We haven't changed anything in here. You want my opinion?" He didn't wait for their answer. "It's the

Piebald Dog on the other side of town. Trying to ruin my business, paint me a fraud with a make believe haunting. The cheek of it!"

"We'll investigate, Mr Chalmer. And in the meantime, we'll have a pint each and the house pie for lunch."

"Right you are." Mr Chalmer stood and dusted his hands on his pants. "Coming up."

"Stefan." He knew what was coming next. "Go and have a look around and report back."

And there it was. He stood up and headed to the bar to start his investigation. When he got back fifteen minutes later, he had managed to cross off most of the obvious reasons and his pint was getting warm next to his pie. Angelica smiled about her fork, raising her eyebrow expectantly.

"There's nothing I can find in or around the premises to account for why their haunting's vanished." He took a long drink and grabbed his knife and fork. "And there's no trauma to resolve, so —"

"Someone's managed to interrupt the pattern somehow. Apparently, he usually becomes visible at the gate, but think about what Mr Chalmer said about Old Pete."

"...He would get off work at the mine and come straight here. So the routine starts at the mine."

"The old, closed mine. I'll give you a chance to eat, then we're off to where Old Pete worked."

The mine had closed decades earlier, due to a mix of safety concerns and lack of profitability. The town had had a resurgence recently with tourism, but the mine was still officially closed-off to the public.

Angelica has never considered herself a member of the public and used her skeleton key to unlock the gate and gesture Stefan through. "We're not going in, just check the upper section. If we need to go deeper, we'll have to apply for an escort to do it. I'm banking on whoever did this not being willing to risk their life over it."

"You're sure it's deliberate?"

"You're not?"

"Well…pretty sure," he agreed. "It's not likely that a tin mine would have anything happen to accidentally interrupt a haunting like this. So yeah, it's probably deliberate. Either someone who has a fear of some kind and felt the need to 'fix' the situation or — or it's business sabotage, like Mr Chalmer thinks."

Angelica smiled slightly, striking a match and lighting up her cigar. "Come on, Boy Wonder, let's go see if we can find our interruption."

The sunlight didn't reach far into the mouth of the mine, but they both carried torches as part of their standard kit. The modern entrance seemed fairly undisturbed, but Angelica pointed out fast enough that back when Old Pete worked the mine, the entrance would have been at a different, more direct location.

The old mine wasn't the creepiest place they'd gone to, but there was something very lonely about it to Stefan's mind. A place that was once the beating heart of the community, that would have had the entire town's worth of people in and out and working in the depths, to be completely empty….

"You can feel it," he murmured. "The loneliness of it, now it's closed."

"Mm." Angelica's smoldering cigar tip waved up and down in his periphery. "You're more sensitive to that sort of thing than me. One of the reasons I asked for you."

"…That's one of the nicest things you've said to me."

"You could do with being less sensitive some of the time." Angelica flicked ash to the side and paused at the rotting wood wall and half-crumbled door set in it. "Next round says this is our interruption point."

"I'm not taking that bet." He moved forward and, under the light of Angelica's torch, felt the door jamb, wiggling it slightly and then lifting it out. "Ah ha."

Someone had dug a shallow furrow under the door jamb and filled it with what looked like table salt. Crude, but effective.

"And there we have it. We'll dig it out, flush it and leave the jamb out."

"Is it our place to free up a repetition?" Stefan sat back on his haunches and looked up at his boss.

"In this situation. The haunting's harmless and this is damaging a man's business. If the mine wanted us to come in and resolve it, it'd be different, but this is a crude attempt to shut down a rival."

Legally, there wasn't a right or wrong, Stefan knew that. And sure, morally, it felt right to put things back and let Old Pete resume his nightly drink. "I suppose…he haunts the pub and the pub want him back."

"*Exactly*. So, dig and flush, Stefan. We can go back and give Mr Chalmer the news that we found the problem and Old Pete should be back in tonight."

"And if he isn't?"

"I'll bet next week's drinks on it being solved."

And if there was one thing Stefan knew, it was not to bet against Angelica where drinks were involved.

Stefan waited in the car, skimming through old case files and witness statements while Angelica finished her cigar, listening to Mr Chalmer's inventive conjecture about the parentage of the owner of the Piebald Dog and the anatomically improbable things he'd do to him if he tried to mess with Old Pete again.

When Angelica got in, she leaned into her seat for a long moment, fingers drumming restlessly on the steering wheel and gaze distant.

"Are you okay?"

"Mm." It was an agreeable sound but not necessarily agreement. "It wasn't what I thought I'd be doing at my age."

Stefan looked to her, but waited in silence.

"I suppose like most of us, I got into this imagining I'd be some paranormal, supernatural guardian of society and the world. Dealing with spies from other realms and threats against nations, not working out why a harmless apparition has stopped turning up to his regular pub."

"Do you regret it?"

"No." She quirked a small smile. "For Mr Chalmer? Old Pete is more important than any secret conspiracy to open portals through the Know. Old Pete keeps his business going and he's like a member of their family. Who the hell am I to say that's not worth my time?"

Stefan nodded, mostly to himself. "And you can't really understand that until you've done the work, been out there working with people."

"Got it. Who knows, maybe we'll get you through that exam after all." Angelica turned the engine over and backed them out of the car park and towards the offices again. "Right, *spot quiz*. Red folder, the case file in there."

Stefan smothered his smile and dug out the folder in question, opening it up. There was a photo of three sullen-looking, identical children and several pictures of a nursery that had been torn apart in a fit of rage and covered in graffiti-like runes.

"All the information you need is in those photos and list of statements on the first page. This family has twins. One of these children is a Dopple and one of them has summoned the Dopple." Angelica glanced at him and smiled. "So … *which* do you think it was?"

"In the Know"

S J MATTHEWS is from South Australia, Australia. She is a disabled, queer writer with two cats, student debt, and an addiction to fountain pens. Her first novel, *The Unknowing*, has just been published by Elephant House Press.

They say: "I was determined to write an entry for at least two of the taxidermy prompts, but I wanted to do something different from my usual work. Stefan and Angelica started out in a story using *The Thin Man* prompt, but then I decided that evil kittens was clearly the only way to go."

Sean Patrick McGinley

Psychopomp, or
Grandeur of the Deranged

ONE THING WAS CERTAIN, that the white kitten had
had nothing to do with it: — it was the black kitten's fault
entirely. But Lucy could not bear to scold the dear fiend. It
stared up at her with its powder-blue eyes, wagging its
mischievous tail in deliberate undulations over the frosted
glass of the coffee table. "O Astor, when will you learn your
manners?" Lucy stooped to collect the porcelain potsherds
strewn across the mahogany floorboards. She looked to the
inquisitive eyes hovering above her. "Now stay still a while,
we don't want you cutting your delicate little paws do we?"
She reached to cradle Astor's tiny head in her caress, but the
swift tomcat darted from her touch, leaping over Lucy's
head and landing on her back. Lucy giggled as she felt
Astor's claws dig into her crimson sweater. Only the pinches
running down her spine let her know that the trickster had
scurried off to find some other misdeed to commit.

Lucy sighed and returned to gathering up the
fragmented china. "Now I know I can trust you to not muck
about, can't I, Gabriel?" Gabriel lounged on the ottoman
just two feet away. He let out a dainty "Miao," prompting
Lucy to approach him and scratch just under his chin. The
bleach-white Siamese squirmed in ecstasy. Its gentle purring
set a similar flutter into Lucy's heart. "Oh, aren't you just
precious?" She pulled her hand away, pitying the kitten's
pleading mew for affection. She rolled up the bottom of her
sweater and scooped the shards into the makeshift pocket.

She made her way to the kitchen garbage bin, doing her best to ignore Gabriel's sulking whines.

She paused a moment next to the bin and laid the shattered fragments on the black quartz island. "Mother really had poor taste," she murmured to herself with a wry smile. In her mind's eye, Lucy returned to that elementary school craft table where she had adorned the cream-white jar with clumsy cobalt flowers. The lilting brush felt fresh in her hands, dragging across the smooth ceramic once again. Three months gone.

She came back to the kitchen counter to find that she had been tracing those movements in reality and had thus suffered a cut from the sharp shards. With her sleeve, Lucy brushed the remnants into the yawning mouth of the garbage bin before she rushed to the sink. As she twisted the knobs to open the faucet's flow she heard a slight mew to her left. There was Astor, stalking towards her on the kitchen counter. "Come to say sorry, are you?" Astor crept closer, his blank stare elucidating nothing. "Look what you've done to me." She offered her bloody forefinger to him, and he approached, eager to lap it up. Lucy felt the abrasive tongue tickle upon her fresh wound. "Oh *now* you're familiar." She chuckled and let Astor lick a little while. Then she shooed him off and began to clean the cut.

He persisted, hovering at her side. He pressed himself against her left arm and shuddered with a full-bodied purr. "You won't fool me again," Lucy murmured to herself and went on with the bandaging. Sensing that he could find no purchase, Astor desisted. He scampered away to hunt another plaything.

Lucy finished dressing the cut and, after dipping into a closet to retrieve dustpan and brush, returned to the coffee table to gather up the remaining specks of porcelain that littered the floor. She bent down and began to brush the lacquered planks when she noticed a small scroll rolled up beneath the table. She picked it up and unrolled the parchment, the unblemished vellum unfolding easily in her grasp. She knew what it would say before she read it:

Don't worry mommy.
We're a family.
We'll be together forever.
—Love, Lucy

If only that child had understood the meaning behind those words….

Lucy raised a balled fist to her forehead and with the cuff of her sweater wiped away the welling tears. "Miao." She turned to Gabriel, who now sat upright. Again he cried to her. She gathered herself and picked up the friendly kitten, cradling it to her bosom. He thrust his head up and licked her cheek, obliterating the salty trickle.

Lucy, still hugging her consoler close, laid down upon the velvet couch. She drew Gabriel to her chest — a soft embrace as she drifted into dream.

Balmy summer zephyrs swaying the bulrushes. The peat-stink of the bay as the boat pulled out of the inlet. Whip-poor-wills dancing in the air above the cliffside, chirping their hungry songs. Father's eyes. The shadow that caught his feet. Crimson-tinged azure. The ruddy, frothing wake. The whip-poor-wills flew, satisfied. No more weekends away. Drop the anchor. No, swim. Pursued. Tiger sharks circling. No, none here, vanished. Float to the headland. Crawl up pebble sands and stow away in the heath. Peek out into the hills: battlefield Lucy. Pink and Black hiding behind the crest, Blues bivouacked in the vale. Caught unawares. She tried to scream out to the feasting commander. Snake out of the reeds wrapped round her throat, comforted her. Total War makes Total Victory for the Pink and Black. Lands seized, borders erased, spoils to the Queen Regent, token to the hostage princess: a lovely crown, a shadowed mind. Screech and howl split her nightmare. Lucy clutched nothing to her chest as she started. A sharp hiss echoed

through the house. Snuffed-out sage meandered to her
nostrils. She rushed up the stairs, lighter in hand, into the
inky blackness of the attic stairwell. The cats ran past her.
She crept upwards, shivering. The frost of her breath hung
before her nose.

Up. Onward. Up.

At the top of it all she saw the smoldering stick of sage
hanging limp in its wooden boat. She flicked the lighter and
reignited the ward. In the dim glow of the flame she saw the
salt line, unbroken, yet disturbed by a paw's fussing. A
hoarse crackle whispered through the door frame, "Which
do you think it was?"

Only the wind and imagination. Return, Lucy. Descend.

Lucy backed down the stairs, watching with intensity the
white smoke wavering in the still air. Safety. Succor. Back to
the living room Lucy lumbered. The culprit awaited her
there, but she could not suss out the guilt. She cast the
thought from her mind: mere curiosity. "Should I feed
them?" She thought. "Do they need to eat?" She set out
three bowls: one for water, one for wet food, one for dry.

Lucy arranged the bowls on the floor of the kitchen
before abandoning the mewing pair. She stepped out the
back door to the garden. Lucy had left it unattended these
past three months, but the consistent rains and rays had
sustained the flowers. She strolled through the rows of lilies,
dahlias, roses, and begonias, their aromas wafting to her
apprehension. Like a ghost through the furrows she floated,
coming eventually face-to-face with the steamed glass of the
greenhouse.

She opened the door and ushered herself inside,
incapable of stopping. The stench offended her, nearly cast
her out of the sanctum, but she, like all things here,
persisted. She fastened the door behind her and continued.

Trains of insects made pilgrimage towards the far end of
the structure. Rotten offal assailed her, carrion airs
enveloping, but on Lucy trudged with her beetle-crushing

heel. There, towering at the edge, was the colossal Titan Arum. Its fleshy spadix loomed eight feet over the surrounding foliage. The vegetable beast sat in its own planter, a throne in truth, erected by Lucy's mother ten years past. For years she had tended this creature, and the care she gave to its well-being was commensurate with that which she gave to Lucy's erudition.

But not once in those ten years had the plant bloomed. Now it stood erect, full, confident, with its scarlet spathe ringing the massive shoot that determined its binomial name. The bloody wreath seemed to breathe with its gentle swaying. Flies danced around it, and scavenging vermin paraded up its body. Soon the fruit would blossom and more would be begotten. One in being, legion in form.

The thought of this stench multiplying racked Lucy's mind with dread. She turned about, surveying the greenhouse's limits, hoping to find a sharp tool. Her eyes fell upon a pair of shears, their steel blades glinting in the late-summer sun. Lucy lunged for the shears, but as she gripped the green rubber, a black claw descended upon her hand. She drew her hand back, blood beginning to rear itself where Astor had struck.

He looked at her, an intense fire behind the cold, blue leer. He let out a harsh hiss. Lucy batted at the air near his head, not wanting to hurt him. He leaped at her head. She covered her face as she fell. When she hit the ground, Lucy at once jumped to her feet again and, fearful of the crawling bugs, whose number had greatly burgeoned in her time since entering the greenhouse, sprinted from the building while fanning out her auburn hair. Relieved that no beetles had burrowed into the locks, she continued, stumbling to the backdoor of her childhood home. "Odd," Lucy thought, "this is Daddy's house…."

Lucy stirred on the couch, unsure this time that she was in the waking world. She lifted herself from the sofa and walked to the kitchen window. She looked upon the garden. The lilies sagged, stems near their breaking point. Rose petals laid withered on the flagstone pathways. The dahlias hung black as pitch. In the greenhouse she could barely make out the image of the limp spadix of the Titan Arum. It would not blossom for her in sooth.

Lucy picked up the wireless phone on the kitchen counter. Her fingers hovered over the number pad for a minute before she endeavored to dial.

BEEP BEEP BEEP

"Hello, this is Dr. Haxan's office. How can I help you?"

"Hi, this is Lucy Beldam. I'd like to come in this afternoon if possible."

"Our records indicate that you've missed your last two appointments. Why is that?"

Lucy covered the mouthpiece and sighed. "I've just been too busy with everything. I desperately need to speak to him today. Is there any chance he could fit me in?"

"Please hold." The cloying pleasantry of the 'waiting room' tunes filtered through the earpiece, numbing Lucy. An eternity passed. The sweet, impatient voice returned. "He has an opening in an hour. Don't miss it this time."

Lucy began to thank the receptionist when she heard the sharp clack of phone hitting holster. She prepared herself for her session: shower, light repast, meditation. She ensured that the kittens' food bowls were still full before setting out. She could not locate the playful cats and with remorse exited the front door without saying goodbye to them. Climbing on top of her bicycle, she bid farewell to the sleeping home.

She rolled down the shaded drive. The willows reached over the whole of the lane, their drooping fingers running through Lucy's hair. Out into the sunlight of the Rhode Island seaside she pedaled. For a few moments, all her worries were whisked away. The bracing wind lifted them from her breast and scattered them down over the edge of the bluff she rode. The foaming sea opened up and swallowed them in azure swells. All that was left was the sunshine, the invigorating inbreath of gentle gusts, and the precipice over the sea. So easy. *L'Appel du vide*. For a few moments she was reminded of what it was to be Lucy Beldam, to inhabit this body for the narrow eternity of her own perception.

She came upon Dr. Haxan's practice drained from her ride. She traipsed inside and sat herself down. The receptionist coughed loudly and asked, "How may I help you?"

Lucy confirmed her appointment, the words falling out of her mouth with no significance. While the receptionist continued her drilling, Dr. Haxan opened the door to his office and invited Lucy inside. "You're early for once," he broached with geniality and a reserved smile.

"I hope it's no burden," Lucy said as she walked past him into the room. She flopped down onto the gray leather couch. She sighed. "I'm sorry if I've gotten your sofa all sweaty, I had to bike here."

"Don't worry about that," Dr. Haxan rebutted. "It's good to get out and exercise. It helps to clear your mind."

"Oh, it's not that I needed the exercise, I seem to have lost my car keys." Lucy chuckled.

Dr. Haxan moved to the armchair opposite Lucy and set himself down. "Well, that's concerning. When did you lose them?"

"Oh, just the other day. It's no big deal, nothing to be worried about."

Dr. Haxan reached into his suit jacket and retrieved a small notebook and pen. He flipped open to a fresh, crisp leaf before closing the pages and looking Lucy in the eye. "How have you been, Lucy? It's been a little while since I've seen you. To be quite frank I was starting to get worried."

"Oh, you know. I'm still getting on. Just a day at a time."

Dr. Haxan let the silence hang for a moment before continuing. "Sara said that you seemed distressed over the phone, almost panicked. Did something happen today?"

A glower flashed over Lucy's countenance. She reined it in, replacing her grimace with an affable grin. "No, nothing in particular. It's just that I haven't come by recently — and I've really been trying to visit, hand to God — and today I decided that I couldn't put it off anymore."

"OK." Dr. Haxan opened his notes again and took up his pen. "How is the medication treating you? You were supposed to come in two weeks ago so we could discuss the effects and whether it was working for you or not."

"It's fine, working fine."

"According to my notes here, your prescription should have run out last week. Are you saying that you were able to get it filled again?"

Lucy bit her lip. "No, no, no. I only meant that, while I was taking it that it worked fine." Dr. Haxan nodded.

"Lucy, I don't want you to think that I'm grilling you or anything like that. This is a place of healing, a place where you can learn to move on. How long has it been since…" Dr. Haxan paused, his right hand palm upwards and rotating in a small circle, "the passing."

"It's been three months since mother died."

"Yes. And grief is still something that we as humans can't define. We can't put it into a neat little box and say 'Here's grief,' and 'Here's comfort or peace.' It takes different forms for each person. It doesn't have a single, identifiable face that we can point to and overcome. I want you to know that this confusion and desperation that you're feeling are all quite natural, that everyone deals with it in their own way. Do you want to tell me what you're facing down right now? What does it look like to you?"

Lucy looked down at the Persian rug spread across the cedar planks. "I still hear her in the attic."

"Grief-induced hallucinations are rare, but they do happen. They arise due to the stress of loss. That's why I prescribed the Valium. It helps to calm you down, but only if you continue your regimen. That's why your hallucinations have resumed. Lucy," Dr. Haxan paused, waiting for Lucy to raise her eyes to his before continuing, "you have to work with me on this. If you don't cooperate then you'll be stuck where you are forever."

"You don't understand, Doctor. The Valium didn't help. Sure, I was calmer when she spoke, but she was still there calling to me to join her. The Valium only calmed me enough that I almost wanted to obey her. The only way I could get the voice to stop was to charm the attic stairwell."

"Lucy, I thought we made progress here. Your mother was not a witch. This whole 'magic' thing you're engaging in is just feeding your delusion. You can't continue on this way. If you want to adjust yourself to the real world you have to accept that."

"How can you say that? You were there when I first heard her. You heard her too. I saw it on your face, even if you won't admit it."

Dr. Haxan shook his head, eyes to the ground. He removed his wire-framed glasses and began polishing the left lens with a silk handkerchief. He looked up to Lucy. "I think I know how you can dispel this notion and truly begin the healing process." Lucy perked up. "You need to go into the attic and see for yourself that none of your fantasies are real. Your mother is gone, Lucy. Go into the attic."

Lucy fell silent, contemplating his suggestion. "But it all seems so real. And the cats, where could they have come from? I remember summoning them. I remember the sigil and the incantation. I remember the smoke. I remember the patters bounding down the stairwell." Dr. Haxan frowned. "Well, maybe I did leave a window open. They could have gotten in like that," Lucy said to the floor.

"Well, Lucy," Dr. Haxan returned his glasses to the bridge of his sharp nose. He crossed his legs, causing bushy black hair to peek out of the edge of his slacks. He flashed a sympathetic smile, his teeth gleaming. "Really, which do you think it was?"

"Psychopomp"

SEAN PATRICK MCGINLEY is a writer from Pennsylvania, in the United States. His short story "Cat and Mouse in Partnership" was published in the anthology *Apocrypha Files II: A Fitting End.*

He says: "This story is an exploration of the duality of perception: your inner world may be wholly discrete from the lives of those surrounding you, but that in no way detracts from its validity. Lucy sees and experiences life in a way that many would call delusional, but to her it is real. Perhaps Lucy is so demented due to grief that she has constructed a world in her own mind where her mother haunts her; or perhaps Lucy truly does exist in a purgatory where her mother acts as a spiritual guide trying to bring her to the Other Side. In any case, it is real to Lucy, and that is what counts."

The Library

"ONE THING WAS CERTAIN, that the white kitten had had nothing to do with it: — it was the black kitten's fault entirely."

Francine Hart looked up to see a man holding a children's book, an illustrated version of *Through the Looking-Glass*. His reading of the one line had been stilted and stumbling.

"It's done. I read what she wanted." said the man, "This book was my wife's. I need to give it back."

The "was" struck a note with Francine. A smidgen of sympathy bubbled up from within, making the man seem less derelict than in her first impression.

"Yes, I can help you with that," she said, taking the hardcover and entering its code into her computer. "It's a lovely book. I'm surprised I don't remember seeing it before."

"Well," said the man, "she had it a long time. It was a great comfort to her, especially when we lost our children."

Francine stopped typing and gazed up at the man. "I'm so sorry," she said. "I can't imagine how terrible that must have been."

The man stood silent, a strange flicker of emotion rippling over his face. "I put it right," he said. "They're all together now."

No results appeared, so Francine once again entered the code. It came up empty. She then noticed the name on the inside cover. "Excuse me, sir," she said, "but I don't believe this book came from our library. It has 'Aurora Public Library' stamped on the inside cover page." The man seemed jarred by this information.

"We met at that library," he said. "She brought the book with her when she came to live with me."

Francine pursed her lips, growing more perplexed by the man's story.

"But not *this* library," she said. "I don't even know where the Aurora Public Library is located."

"Illinois," he said; "I brought her from Illinois. I gave her a good life, but the book made her troublesome. I have to give it back."

The man was growing agitated. It made Francine nervous, as there were not many people in the library at that particular time of day. She offered up her sweetest smile.

"Well, maybe I can help you somehow. Could I start by getting your wife's name?"

"She made me call her Alice," he said.

"That is rather unusual, Mr…?" Francine left the hint hanging, but the man either didn't notice or was choosing to ignore it. He hitched up his trousers and tightened his belt a notch.

"Bob," he said. "I'm just Bob to everybody. My wife was Mandy."

"Okay, Bob," said Francine, "and did she have a maiden name?"

"A maiden name?" he replied, with a blank stare.

"Her name before she was married," said Francine. "Many women keep it, nowadays."

"You won't try to trick me if I tell, will you?" said Bob. "Like not taking the book 'cause I had the name wrong or something?"

"No, no," said Francine, adding a theatrical chuckle, "consider it returned. But it would be good to have some history when I arrange to have it sent back to Aurora."

Bob stood in silence; a brooding silence. "Mandy Kent," he whispered. "She was Mandy Kent."

Something rippled in the oceanic depths of Francine's middle-aged brain, but she couldn't get it to swim to the surface.

"If you don't mind," she said, "I need to use a different computer to access information about the Aurora Public Library. Could you wait here for a moment?"

Bob knitted his brows, then turned and walked in silence to a bench located in an alcove off to the side. Francine got up slowly and slid the book under her arm. She tried not to hurry, which is what she felt like doing.

"I won't be more than a few minutes," she said, as she made her way to an office at the back of the library.

Francine slipped through the door and sat in front of an aging PC. She pulled up Google and input "Mandy Kent." A number of references appeared, but a September 14, 2003 article from the *Chicago Tribune* caught her eye:

It's been five years since ten year old Mandy Kent disappeared without a trace. The young daughter of Max and Melissa Kent was last seen borrowing a book from the Aurora Public Library, only one block over from the family home. Last Sunday, at the opening of a children's reading room named in her honour, Mandy's family spoke of having hope that she will one day be returned to them.

"Our prayers for her safe return only grow stronger," said her mother. "We will never give up on our little girl."

It took every bit of Francine's self-control to stop herself from vomiting. Tears formed in her eyes and she wiped them away with a violent swipe of her sleeve. Her mind was flooded by a wave of unwanted images. *Children*, for Christ's sake. How old was Mandy when she had *children*?

Francine stared at the book, its existence now a wonder to her, its power bordering on miraculous. When Francine came back to herself, she was gripping the edge of the desk so hard her knuckles were white.

"I have to move," she muttered, suddenly beset by an

unbearable feeling of heaviness. "I have to call the police."

Francine stretched out a trembling hand and placed it on the book, praying it might be a talisman, something that could break the spell that held her. The movement of her hand gave her momentum, a rhythm that activated the rest of her frame. She wriggled forward and came to her feet. She reverently picked up the book and leafed through the first few pages. To her surprise, a scrawled note was penciled into the margin. Francine turned the book so she could decipher the blocky handwriting: *Mandy is o.k. Alice will look after her.*

A couple of pages later was another one: *I am safe in here.*

Francine flipped through the entire book, her eyes blurring with tears. Near the end, written in large letters, was a last entry:

I am Mandy Kent. Bob never ever got me. Don't be afraid of Bob. Bob can only hurt babies. The babies are under the apple tree.

Bob watched the librarian all the way to the door through which she had disappeared. It's a rabbit hole, he thought to himself, the book will come out the other side and I'll have to take it home with me. He shuddered at the thought. Alice had made it clear what would happen if he didn't return it. Bob was terrified of being haunted by her for the rest of his life.

It had taken all his willpower to walk into this place. Bob didn't like books, they made him think of his mother and her casual brutality. The books she read to Bob had made him fear the burning fires of hell, made him everywhere see lost and suffering souls screaming in a sin stoked inferno. He had killed his mother when he was seventeen and stuffed her body in a culvert.

Bob got up and walked back into the reception area. The library lady was taking too long and his head was starting to bang in the bad way it did when his Momma had hurt him all those years ago. He knew only one way to make it stop.

He started walking towards the rabbit hole.

Francine reached for the phone. The charging stand was empty. She swiveled to look about the room, hoping to find the handset on an adjacent desk. The door swept open as she did so, and Bob came through, closing it after himself.

"Is there a problem?" he said.

Francine had seen crazy people before, but not murderous, crazy people, to which tribe she was sure Bob belonged. She knew she couldn't run.

"Yes, Bob, there might be," she said, managing to keep her voice level. "It seems the book is quite long overdue. There is a fine to be paid."

"Why do I have to pay?" he said. "It was her book. I never looked at it."

Francine picked the book up from the desk and held it out towards Bob. He cringed like it was a lance of fire. She took a step forward.

"I think you better keep it, Bob."

"No, no, no!" he howled. "She said it had to come back or she would come for me! You have to take it!"

A current of fear shimmered across Francine's belly. She felt the heaviness settling on her once again, but pushed against it. Her brain was deluged with wild thoughts and visceral impulses. One thought crystallized, breaking free of the turbulent debris that cluttered her sub-conscious mind. It felt like it came through her ears, but she knew it could only be in her head: *Don't be afraid of Bob.*

"Did you hear Alice, just now?" she said.

"No, and you can't either," said Bob. "You can't because she died three days ago."

Francine put the book down and leaned on the desk to steady herself. "She said you buried the babies under the apple tree."

Bob's face paled.

"How?" he stammered. "How can you know that?"

When Bob's hand came out of his trouser pocket, it was clutching an ugly, bone-handled hunting knife. Francine urinated on herself, the hot liquid seeping through her underwear and running down her leg to form a jaundiced puddle around her feet. When Bob crouched and began inching forward, Francine began fearing for her life.

"Why didn't you just take the book?" he said. "Alice wouldn't have said anything to you, if you did. You're no Alice, lady."

Francine turned and stumbled against the desk. Her hands came down on the book, 10 by 14 inches of beautiful hardcover. As Bob moved into his final approach, his foot slipped on the urine-splattered floor. Francine gripped the book in both hands and spun towards him, her considerable bulk creating a torque that turned the lovely children's book into a deadly weapon. Francine had never read about hand-to-hand combat, so was unaware of how lucky she was when the corner of the book struck Bob in his carotid sinus, just northeast of his Adam's apple. The disrupted baroreceptors informed the brain it was having a stroke and Bob crumpled to the floor, soon to be dead.

"Was that me, or Alice?" shrieked Francine, as she straddled Bob's inert body and began pounding on his face with the book. "Was that me, or Alice?"

She was still pounding with the tattered remains of *Through the Looking-Glass* when the only other person in the library came through the door. Eighty-seven year old Mrs. Adelaide Snipes, life-long library cardholder, had never in all her days come upon such a terrifying scene. In the weeks to follow, even when it became clear that Francine Hart was a hero and not a crazed lunatic, Mrs. Snipes could no longer bring herself to come to the library.

The story of Mandy Kent unfolded in the local media; the remains of three infants and one twenty-nine year old female were found buried under an apple tree on rural property belonging to Robert Martin Gravely, local handyman, now deceased. An underground bunker, and evidence of prolonged incarceration, was found under the garage.

Mrs. Snipes died three weeks later, fretting away the last portion of her life trying to unravel the cryptic question put to her by Francine Hart. Francine never returned to the library, and she spent the rest of her days in a facility of an entirely different sort, a place where she continued to obsess over the event, even publicly acting it out if she were taken off her medication.

"Was that me, or Alice?" Francine had screamed over and over, as she pounded on Bob's face.

When she noticed Mrs. Snipes, she gently put the book aside.

"Was that me, or Alice?" she said, blood-splattered, in her best librarian's voice — "Which do you think it was?"

"The Library"

NED HERBERT BOYDEN is trying to feed and shelter a family of four in a wildly-overpriced city in British Columbia, Canada. His story "A Certain Degree of Latitude" was published in *Shadows Express* (Fall, 2010).

He says: "My co-worker was unwillingly assigned to the library of the law firm I work for, so I jokingly said I would write a story for this contest called, 'The Girl Who Went to the Library.' I tossed it three times. I credit my writers group for helping me break through when someone posted an article on 'How to Write Great Villains.' Twenty-five cups of coffee later, the villain was a person — an ugly one, but with a backstory."

Shyamal R Swamy

Literary Kittens

One thing was certain,

That the white kitten had had

nothing to do with it: — it was the black kitten's fault entirely.

He pounces on every fluffy thought, every dust bunny of an

idea, and spreads himself on the pages; leaving a trail of

black strands, scattered in Latin shapes to convey…

To convey something Usually oh so profound

With every tip tap of the

keys, The

black kitten prances off, To fill the

pages, in his chase of that fluffy thought, that dust bunny of an

idea. But little did you notice the white kitten that counters his every

step. She deftly moves to block his path, She pounces on him, Forces him to take

new paths, To fit new shapes. He, always jumping over her. She, always creating

chasms for him. They entangle in graceful chaos, to create the pages you pour over

But, where did the meanings come from? The black strands may stand out to you now,

But would you see them on a black page? The strands or spaces? The black kitten

or the white kitten? These lines? Or

these spaces?

Words? Chasms?

Which do you

think it was?

"Literary Kittens"

SHYAMAL R SWAMY is a student from Victoria, Australia. Her poem "Serenity: A Gift of My Poetry," has been published in the book *For Poets, by Poets*, edited by Shanon Norman (2013), and her poems "That Question," "Impossible Thank You," "My friendship," and "Innocence" have all been published in *The Times of India*.

She says: "It was around 1:00 am and I was awake looking for writing contests to shake off my writer's block. I found the rules for this contest and thought, *this will be fun!* On reading further I realized the deadline was in few hours…."

Serpent King

"ONE THING WAS CERTAIN, that the white kitten had had nothing to do with it: — it was the black kitten's fault entirely. The Serpent King would not have found me if it had not been for the black kitten. I was lying on the edge of the river, my legs dangling over the bank, my feet cooling in the river water. My only companions were the kittens, we were alone together as we had been so many times before. I was unearthing within myself a pleasure that was all my own. A pleasure that would come of being wed to my own reflection in the water of that river. I, as you know, have steadfastly refused to marry any of the suitors my parents or brother have dragged forth."

I am sitting in a small, ornate chair across from my lady while she tells this story. The black kitten is currently sitting on the ledge of the single, small window, blocking what little natural light enters the circular room. The white kitten is not easily visible, camouflaged by a pillow, it's small body curled around upon itself. She gets up and walks over to each of the kittens in turn, petting them gently and murmuring words of comfort, to herself or them I am not certain. The black kitten pushes his head up into her hand, maximizing the effect of her attention. The white kitten makes a small noise and snuggles further into the pillow. The lamps, hung at regular intervals, burn weakly and cast long shadows, which continue to take on a life of their own. As she walks around the room, the shadows move with her and she interacts with them in a dance that is all her own.

"Indeed, my lady, the ceremony will take place

tomorrow. Your father has commanded it."

"I am no longer his to command. His reign is finished, it will not last the day."

"That is treason, my lady."

"It is truth, no less."

"This kingdom lives faithfully by the scriptures, it will last a long while yet."

She gives a wild, bitter laugh, the shadows arching high, becoming a heckling crowd. "Ah yes, the bastardized version that is preached to us. I have read the stone, seen it with my own eyes."

"The stone is lost, nobody has seen it for many generations."

"The stone is a short distance away down the forbidden path."

"The forbidden path? No…no, no, my lady."

She waves me off, returns to her seat. The shadows fall to the floor, huddling around her. The white kitten wakes up, stretches and yawns, jumps down off the bed and comes padding over, gracefully leaping onto her lap and curling itself back into a ball, instantly asleep again. The black kitten turns, small black eyes glowing, and hisses.

"It will be soon now," she says.

She lays her head back against the chair, closing her eyes and idly caressing the white kitten. "We have jumped too far ahead, you understand nothing."

"My lady, I am here to understand."

"You are a spy, nothing more. I will tell you my tale, it will come to life for you. I wonder, will you survive the ordeal?" She opens one eye and glares at me, then shuts it, her dainty mouth curving into a small smile. "Where was I?"

"The edge of the river my lady."

"Yes. The white kitten was beside me, always the more dependent of the two. Gifts from my sisters, the balance of light and dark, an equalizing force." That bitter laugh again, then: "More than they know. The black kitten was off cavorting around, brewing up mischief. I had learned to let him be, he always returned on time and appeared to be immune to danger."

"That sounds like neglect my lady."

"I am not their keeper, they are mine. We have been going to the river bank since they were weeks old, I had my preparations to do for the ceremony."

"Is that what you were doing on the day in question?

"No, you are not listening. I was enjoying the moment, the feel of my body on the sand, the sun on my skin. I had removed my outer layers and was lying only in my shift, which was pulled up past my knees, my arms spread wide, my fingers tracing patterns in the sand."

"My lady, if you had been seen."

Her head jerks up, her eyes stormy. The white kitten gives a small hiss in protest, the black kitten turns his back to look out the window again. The shadows start swirling around her chair, I lift my feet to avoid contact with them. "If you insist on interrupting me, I will not continue."

"I beg your pardon, my lady. I will refrain until the end."

She rests her head back, the shadows calming as she does so. "I heard the familiar sound of the black kitten racing through the underbrush along the path leading to the river. His small paws hit the gravel at the edge of the beach, causing them to rattle and collide, then he was beside me on the warm sand. He curled up by my ear as he always does, his purr thundering through his small body and reverberating through mine. It is a most comforting sensation." She lifts her legs, "footstool." The shadows obey, pushing the small stool over from the bed until it is below her feet. "Massage."

One shadow detaches itself from the others and circles around her legs and feet, kneading them as she makes small sounds of pleasure. I turn my head away, embarrassed by the intimacy of the moment.

"You always were squeamish, get ready for your skin to crawl." Her voice has softened, a sultry quality now tinges the edges of her words, causing prickles on the back of my neck and a bead of sweat to form, trickling down the inside of my shirt.

"I am the court scribe, I have heard all manner of misdemeanors in my time."

"Really? We shall see."

"I am confident, my lady."

She makes a snort of derision, continues with her tale: "The black kitten had not returned alone, I did not hear the approach of the other, only felt the pressure on my skin, then the weight of him on my body. I was consumed by him, his length enveloping me before I had time to react. He explored every inch of me and I lay still, I knew better than to fight such a force. I kept my eyes closed, believing the sight of him would cause fear to roil in my stomach, induce me to lash out in a stupid act of self-preservation. He slithered off me and I thought he was gone, until I felt his tongue, flicking along each part of me, until I had been fully tasted and tested. I admit I moaned in pleasure at times, I had never been touched in such a way."

I swallowed, my throat dry, my pen hovering over the scroll, a dead instrument. I shook my head to clear my thoughts but the image she painted was vivid. I admonished myself, I needed to regain control, remember my station in life. She picked up the white kitten and gently placed him on the floor, stood up and walked behind my chair.

"Oh, you've made an error, your scroll is quite a mess. Looks like you will need to start again." She bends down, her lips right against my ear, "Unless you want to ravish me now?"

"No…no, my lady…I am well, let us continue…*please*."

She stands up, laughing at me, and walks over to the bed while I fumble with my quills, dropping the scroll and knocking over the ink bottle. She lies down on the bed, stretching her body luxuriously. I stop and watch her, forgetting every rule that has been hammered into my feeble skull since I was a child.

"I believe I have unsettled you."

She does not look at me but lies on the bed and allows her hands to roam over her body. I am entranced, forgetting my scroll, the ink spreading a path across the floor, staining my shoe. I stand and take a step towards her. Both kittens race towards me, their little fangs bared, the shadows rising behind them, an immovable barrier.

"I belong to the Serpent King." Her hands circle her abdomen and pause there, "I now carry his child and it is death for another to desire me. I have gone to him every night for the past two months and he has done things to me that others could never imagine." She rolls over onto her front, rests her head on her hands, looks over at me and winks. "Do you know he can alter shape and take on a human form? When he does this, his eyes are emeralds, his body glitters in sunlight and glows by moonlight. His snake skin pattern stretches into a faint tattoo that can be traced in a continuous pattern around his body. He has bed me in all his forms, I am his gift and his life. He will have me, and I will bear his heir. This kingdom is finished, it has denied him his rightful place, it has rewritten the scriptures and devoured itself on power and greed."

A shadow rears up in front of me, extending a limb and pushes me back in my seat, where I sprawl over the edge. Another shadow races around my legs, strapping them to the legs of the chair and a third takes my arms behind me. I am unable to right myself and so sit there, bolted and tilted, a puppet on a string.

She sits up on the bed, her hands ripping her bodice apart, shredding the sleeves of her dress. She stands and starts to walk the room again, the kittens following.

"You will all feel his wrath now. My pious father with his petty quarrels and fat incompetence. My mother, the wench, who perhaps should have come clean about the true nature of my parentage. Let us not forget my brother, with incestuous designs on all his sisters. He has not been able to touch me, not in my supposed virgin state. The only reason, I would wager, he is so determined to see me marry. The weak husbands of my darling sisters turning a blind eye each time he beds them."

My head is at an odd angle, a crick forming in my neck, but I must respond to her, attempt to divert the disaster she is courting.

"It is tradition, my lady, as written in the scriptures."

"Lies and treachery. You forget, I have read the original. They preach us nothing but a glorified misinterpretation of the truth." She is continuing to work at her dress, shredding it apart so that it falls around her in tatters. "So now we come to it, my incarceration in this tower. Who found out about my nightly visits to the Serpent King? Three days and nights I have been here. Who betrayed me? Who is responsible?"

I make a small noise in the back of my throat and she waves her arm in a circle. The shadows release me, and I tumble onto the ground along with the chair.

"Is it a betrayal?" She is muttering to herself now, pacing back and forth in front of the window. My legs have gone numb from the pressure of the shadow and I struggle to sit upright. Before I can make the effort to stand, she rushes over to me, kneels so her face is level with mine and I am looking into her blazing, green eyes.

"Which one, dear scribe? A betrayal or conspiracy? Are they planning to allow me my marriage to my reflection tomorrow or are they going to make me a sacrifice? Which do you think it was that led me up here, will lead you all to your deaths?"

With that I hear the first whistle and roar, the ground shakes and the entire castle shifts and moves. She stands up and crosses over to the window, throwing back her head and laughing with a manic glee. I scramble to my feet and stumble over to see, the tingling sensation along my legs causing me to walk with a lurching gait. I peer out the window and see a man, his skin glittering in the sun, his emerald eyes burning bright. The walls around the castle are covered in snakes, a swirling mass of them, smothering guards and pulling them over the edge, where they fall to the ground. The guards remain lifeless while the snakes return to climb the wall again. Another whistle and roar, a larger impact, I hold the ledge to keep my balance.

"Time to run, little scribe," her lips barely move, the words coming out of her mouth in a hiss.

I start to back up and she pursues me, her face a mask of rage and hatred, her words chasing me, "Which do you think it was, scribe, *betrayal* or *conspiracy*?"

I turn and bolt for the door, taking one last look before I wrench it open and collapse into the hallway, her voice thundering this final question after me. I crawl down the hallway before staggering to my feet and running. I have trouble focusing on where I am going, my vision transfixed by the image of her standing in the middle of the room, her dress in disarray, the shadows spinning circles around her. The kittens flanking her on either side, their small bodies arched, the hair on their backs standing straight up, their small faces contorted into hisses. Her question echoes in the chaos of a building being torn asunder.

Which do you think it was? Which do you think it was? Which do you think it was?

"Serpent King"

SAMANTHA JOHNSON is an administrative assistant from Alberta, Canada. She has a degree in Biochemistry and a diploma in Chemical Engineering Technology. Her submission to the Parker contest, "The Jellybean Bet," received honorable mention. "Serpent King" is her first published story.

She says: "I wrote this story the day before the contest closed. Once I finally came up with an idea — a woman locked in a circular room — the story took only a few hours to write. My primary intent was to ensure neither the story nor the kittens were cute and cuddly."

Rhiannon Pickstone

The Clouds and the Stars

ONE THING WAS CERTAIN, that the white kitten had had nothing to do with it: — it was the black kitten's fault entirely. I felt a drop of water run down my skin. The kittens. Maybe without them, it all would have been different. When I met Albert, I knew it was the best thing that could ever happen to me. We talked a lot, mostly about the clouds at day and the stars at night. We listened only to old music and watched only old films and we both thought we were in love. I did not really care for love before, but Albert made me understand what a wonderful thing it could be. He made me see and understand a lot of things. For the first time in my life, I understood why there were so many poems about the way the wind moves the trees. Everything was suddenly so beautiful. Albert proposed to me eventually and of course I said yes, and we celebrated in a small circle of people we both called friends because Albert knew their name, their occupation, and their relationship status. We talked about getting children but in the end we both decided on kittens. One black, one white. Darkness and light. Albert and me. Me and Albert. We had been happy for a while, in harmony with each other, but when we got the kittens something changed. When Albert came home, he first greeted the black kitten, then the white one and only then me. Albert talked about them all the time. I couldn't understand that. I liked them, sure, after all one likes tiny things, doesn't one? But I didn't see why Albert made such a fuss about them. He even gave them names (which I thought was unnecessary, after all we could just call them black and white) and he abbreviated those names and called them love and darling. He called me love and darling before.

I wasn't jealous, after all one isn't jealous of kitten, mere stupid animals, now is one? But we fought after we got the kittens. I screamed at Albert, he just didn't respond, or he hid behind some sort of nature magazine. The kittens being there wherever we fought just fueled my angriness, especially when Albert tried to shush me to not scare them. There was something about these small animals that made me angrier and Albert more depressed. We fought about our never-changing daily life, about the kittens, and finally we fought about the clouds and the stars. I didn't understand what he loved about all those things anymore. I didn't understand his talking about the way the wind moves the trees. One day I saw him. He thought I was away, but I saw him. In the car, with a woman. I thought that she looked terrible. It pained me a little bit, but not too much. At first, I wanted to do it as well. He had a very good-looking friend, and it would be fun. He wouldn't know what hit him and it probably would hurt him so much more for he really seemed to like that friend. But the friend was one of the good ones. He kindly rejected me and out of kindness ran to Albert to tell him all about it. Albert was so furious. I laughed a lot during his rage talk about how I could possibly even attempt to do such a thing, and what a monster I was. I stopped laughing when he called me psychotic. Crazy bitch he said. I told him that I saw him, and it was his time to laugh — at me! He didn't have any right to laugh at me. After all it was all his fault. He talked about what a great woman that bitch was. Prettier than me, he said. He couldn't stand my face anymore. And when I talked…. How can any human being be so stupid? The kittens got upset during our fight, they always did. But while the white kitten hid as far away as possible, the black kitten hopped on the table and seemed to watch our fight. She whimpered from time to time. But she stared at me with her eyes wide open. I began to feel uneasy. Albert continued to laugh, scream at me.

Insult me, that bastard. What right did he have to behave that way? We used to love each other but he had to throw it away, because he was a man. Because he had *needs*. It could have been so amazing, perfect, if he hadn't done that. I could never forgive him that. The black kitten didn't move. The darkness, I thought. Albert didn't stop. Why didn't he stop? All I could see was the kitten's dark fur. It would be better without Albert; my life would be better. The kitten meowed. We were in the kitchen. My life still could be good. I had many years left. Albert kept screaming at me. I don't quite remember what happened next. Just my counting. Once. Twice. Thrice. *Done.*

I moved to another house. Took the white cat with me. She hadn't done anything, she just hid away. I couldn't be mean to her just because of what her companion did. I left the black kitten. Probably dead by now. A young boy always came to my house to watch the white cat when I was gone. He told me about some strange happenings in another neighbourhood. Some people think that he is dead, he said. Others say he ran away. His wife was just a terrible woman. He could have killed himself. He asked me what I thought had happened. "Suicide, or running away? — which do you think it was, miss?" he asked, staring up at me. He had blue eyes just like Albert. I stared at them and was reminded of the sky, of a faraway place with clouds and stars. I didn't quite remember whether I had been happy then. I don't quite know whether I am happy now. The boy waited, his blue eyes not leaving me, but I knew that this was a question he had to wait on being answered forever. Suicide or running away. I had to stop myself from laughing aloud. Which do you think it was?

"The Clouds and the Stars"

RHIANNON PICKSTONE is a student from Leverkusen, Germany. "The Clouds and the Stars" is her first published story.

She says: "I knew the novel *Alice in Wonderland* and I wanted to write a story that is very different from the original novel."

Curses

ONE THING WAS CERTAIN, that the white kitten had had nothing to do with it: — it was the black kitten's fault entirely. It started very innocently, a few of the usual taps of Mavis' slippers on the floorboards. Scratches and bumps of the kittens skittling along the floor. Then it was a crash and a shout, YOU BLOODY THING, and the metallic sound of a bowl spinning and slowing to a stop upside down.

Ivor came rushing into the kitchen to pick Mavis up from the floor.

THAT BLOODY CAT, IVOR, IF I'VE TOLD YOU ONCE I MUST HAVE TOLD YOU A THOUSAND TIMES GET IT OUT OF MY HOUSE.

Whenever something happened — you know, the blind spontaneously falling from the kitchen window; Ivor's money going missing from his wallet; Mavis taking a bad fall on the front step — the black kitten got the blame.

This time the cats' bowl had spilled all over the floor. I could tell because water was starting to seep through into the cellar.

Ivor's footsteps came into the kitchen. Mavis was still hitting the roof and, in his usual cooing way, Ivor was trying to calm her down while ushering her out into the living room.

It's alright love, I'll sort it. I'll clean it up.

But Mavis wouldn't calm down. I'm sure she stood her ground, glowering in the doorframe.

WHAT ARE WE GOING TO DO ABOUT THIS

BLEEDIN CAT?

Kneeling on the floor, Ivor started to mop up the spilt water. Instead of one localized spot, a whole seam of it was dripping smack, smack, smack onto the concrete floor.

It's no use crying over spilt milk, love.

I'M NOT CRYING OVER SPILT MILK! IT'S THAT BLOODY CAT! I WANT RID OF IT.

This was the same patter I and M rolled out each time something went wrong in the house. The end result was always the same.

I'll think of something, love.

This is another thing that was certain, Ivor would always try earnestly to think of "something" to do with "that bloody cat" but, it became apparent, Ivor would never do anything.

Hearing all this from my unique vantage point beneath them I decided that it was up to me, in fact, to do "something" about the black cat.

After making her a cup of tea, Ivor managed to settle Mavis down. But, for the rest of the day, whenever she came to cross the black kitten, Mavis would stop dead in her tracks, and HISS loudly at the little thing.

Gosh, their floorboards were thin.

In the weeks I had hidden away down there in the couple's cellar, I had grown accustomed to their daily routine. At 9 o'clock they both went upstairs to bed. At around 9:30 one of them would flush the toilet sending a rush of water down the pipes. Then from 10 onwards there wouldn't be another sound until the 4am bathroom run.

Though this routine was the same each night, I had never before had the courage to creep up and enter the couples' house in the dead of night. I had only done it in the day when I knew both of them would be out at the supermarket, or the time they went away for the weekend.

It was about 11pm when I entered the house.

My usual entry was through the kitchen window. Unless it was raining, the couple would leave it ajar. Opening it as wide as it would go, I could, with some effort, slide through and on to the counter at the other side.

This is what I did that evening. Only in the dark, I hadn't noticed the cutlery drying on the side. My feet swiped the whole lot onto the floor.

IVOR!

Clearly, I had woken Mavis.

What? What is it, love?

Mavis, of course, blamed the black kitten.

IT'S AT IT AGAIN! DOWNSTAIRS. I BET IT'S MADE A RIGHT MESS!

I didn't move an inch until I heard the floorboards creak under Ivor's footsteps. Like a shot, I was in the pantry, pressed tightly against soup tins and teabags.

Ivor padded down the stairs in his slippers and switched on the kitchen light. Through a crack in the pantry door I saw my — can I call him neighbour? — for the first time. Balding with white hair and glasses, he was the bland, stock image of "the elderly gentleman next door."

Holding his knee, he bent down to pick up the knives and forks, then placed them back on the side where he had left them before.

Here, puss puss puss. I watch him stoop down to check beneath the cabinets for any sign of the two kittens. *Where are yeh now?* My hands had grown sweaty, and I gripped the knife as tightly as I could. C'mon, little ones.

He was now looking for any gaps under the door which they might've squeezed through. Barely a nose-length away from me, I tried my best to regulate my breath; to dissolve and blend in seamlessly with the shadows in the cupboard.

Bizarrely, time seemed to slow down. So much so that I could count all the white hairs of Ivor's eyebrows, explore the deep ravines of his heavily wrinkled face, figure out the topography that made this man an individual, recognisable to those he loved anywhere in the world.

There was a scuffle on one of the shelves behind me.

Though I could not turn my head far enough to discern the thing making the sound, at that moment I knew, and Ivor heard, it was one of the kittens.

Which do you think it was?

"Curses"

BEAU JACKSON is a writer from England. "Curses" is her first published story.

She says: "I made a promise to myself that I would enter writing competitions this year, but it's only thanks to my girlfriend that I have managed to keep that promise. Known by us as 'The Kitten Story' I wrote my tale between articles at work and on trains from home to the city. The final submission was made about 5 minutes before the deadline on intermittent station wi-fi. Thank you, Kirstie, for telling me (over and over) that I should go for it."

What Happened to Prissy McGibbon

ONE THING WAS CERTAIN, that the white kitten had had nothing to do with it: — it was the black kitten's fault entirely.

My neighbor, Priscilla McGibbon, sat at my favorite chair at my table in my kitchen, drinking the tea I'd poured for myself out of my favorite cup. She'd swept right in, made herself comfy, and made me wait, the story of her current traumatic situation unfurling somewhat incoherently in between dainty sips of Sleepy Time.

"Will you come over and take a look?" she asked. With a trembling hand, Prissy — sometimes I call her Prissy and sometimes I call her Cilly, and both nicknames fit quite snugly around her personality — placed my favorite cup on its saucer with more of a clatter than I would've liked.

"Well, Priscilla," I said, as she leaned towards me, each of her features working together to form a mask of feminine helplessness, "I don't know anything about cats. I didn't even know you *had* cats."

She blinked rapidly, like a baby forest critter seeing the big, scary world for the first time. Reaching out, she placed her hand on mine. I don't particularly care for being touched.

"Please," she said. "At least come over and take a peek at what devastation that kitten has wrought."

I sighed. Yesterday, she'd needed me to fix her leaky sink. The day before, her porch swing creaked. I swear, the

165

woman was trying her darndest to cast me in the role of her handyman, though I am not a man nor am I particularly handy.

"Can't it wait until tomorrow?" I asked.

"I baked a peach cobbler," she said. "And have a pint of vanilla ice cream in the freezer."

It was much too late in the evening for *à la mode* to be appropriate, but no matter what time of day, I could not turn down cobbler.

She squeezed my fingers. "I don't know what I would do without you, Irma. You're my best friend."

Lacking any other friends, I supposed she was mine, too, if only by default. She stood and smoothed down her skirt, adjusting each ruffle so it was just so. I slipped on my shoes and followed her across the street.

"Where are these kittens?" I asked, planning to make sure they weren't rabid before calling around at dawn's first light to find them suitable homes. Other than baking, Priscilla is not fit to care for any living thing.

"Right there," she gestured towards the mantle, while looking in the other direction.

Over the fireplace sat — and I should've known this — two porcelain figurines, one of a black kitten, one of a white kitten.

"It is quite obvious who the guilty party is," Priscilla said, shielding her eyes with her hand, but peeking through her fingers. "You see how the white kitty has a genteel and sweet expression, while the black one smirks mischievously. They both looked genteel and sweet when I bought them from the resale shop. What I think happened is, sometime during the day, the black kitty was possessed by some kind of evil spirit and."

I held up both hands, as stop signs, not in surrender. "You just put me a chunk of that cobbler in some Tupperware, Priscilla. It's past my bedtime and I'm going home."

"No!" she cried, on me like a tick, looping her arm around mine, locking me at her side. "You haven't even seen what it did."

She pressed her forehead against my shoulder. "It's in the dining room. Be careful."

She let me go and gave me a push.

I rolled my eyes. I have got to let this woman stop taking advantage of my generous spirit.

I stalked to the dining room and gasped.

One of my feet, the one already over the threshold, dangled over thin air like I was a cartoon character.

I yanked my leg back and lost my balance, falling backwards onto the shag carpeting.

"I told you to be careful!" Priscilla scrambled to my side and helped me up.

"What in tarnation happened to your dining room floor?" I winced and though it's not ladylike, I rubbed my backside, which would be sore tomorrow for sure.

I craned my neck, sticking my head and only my head into the dining room, where most of the floor was gone, leaving only a black hole where it used to be.

Priscilla grabbed my arm again and whispered into my ear. "I'm telling you. The kitten was possessed by an evil spirit and —" she cupped her hand against my cheek and dropped her voice even further — "it opened up a portal to *hell*."

I glanced back towards the living room, towards the shag carpeting, overwhelmed by the sudden urge to lie down and take a nap right then and there. The only thing that kept me from doing so was the real and present fear I'd wake up to this unhinged woman standing over me with a knife pointed at my throat.

"Forget the cobbler. I'm going home," I said, wrestling my arm away from her vise grip.

"You can't just leave me here!" she said, every word

more shrill than the last. "The devil himself might come up and steal my soul!"

"Cilly McGibbon," I straightened my shoulders and pulled myself up to my full five foot one-and-a-half inches. I hadn't been quite so annoyed with her since she suggested we form the SIS of Bloom Street Club. SIS standing for Spinsters In Solidarity, in case you couldn't work that acronym out for yourself. "That there is *not* a portal to hell. It's a portal to your basement. This house is approximately five thousand years old. The whole thing's probably rotten or eaten by termites. Tomorrow you — and by you, I mean you and not me — will call some repairmen and get some estimates."

"Can I spend the night at your house?" she squeaked.

"No," I said, and not just because of the possibility of waking up with a knife at my throat. "Sleepovers are for children." And sometimes even though there are walls and a road between us, I swear I could hear Priscilla talking in her sleep and she had very vivid dreams about making babies with Clark Gable, though he is long dead and so are her eggs. She dressed like she was a housewife in a 1940s television show, but there were some X-rated sugar plums dancing in that woman's head.

"But, but … what if it *is* a portal to hell and something escapes during the night and drags me back down to the underworld with it?" she asked. "I can't stay here."

"Well, then, you better call Motel Six and see if there's any room left at the inn," I said. She responded with a quivering lip.

Thank goodness this house was built long before anyone had ever uttered the words "open concept." I marched over and slammed the door to the dining room shut. Then I dragged over a chair and pushed it up under the knob. "There. You're safe. Good night."

"Will you at least take the black kitten with you?"

I rolled my eyes again. "Yeah, all right, whatever." I

swiped it on the way out.

I went home and crawled into bed, feeling slightly guilty about leaving poor Priscilla alone and scared, but not guilty enough to do anything about it. I fell asleep and tumbled into terrible nightmares, which I supposed served me right.

I woke up the next morning, narrowly escaping a fire-breathing dragon. My heart pounded. I knew it was only a dream, but I'd just watched Priscilla get singed to death, frilly apron and all going up in flames.

"Ouch," I winced, alert and aware. My wrist stung as if I'd gotten it tangled up in a briar patch. I turned it over to see scratches. "Well, what in the world?"

My eyes strayed to the figurine of the black kitten sitting on my night stand where I'd set him without much thought. I had to be imagining things, but his smirk appeared even more mischievous.

I scrambled out of bed and without even changing out of my nightgown, hauled rump over to Priscilla's, as any good friend would do. I let myself in with the spare key she kept stashed underneath the welcome mat. The stillness overwhelmed me.

"Priscilla?" I called, though I knew in my gut she would not answer. Priscilla's place felt like our family's beach house did when I was a child, the first time we opened the doors after it had been left empty all winter.

"Priscilla?"

From the entranceway, I could see the dining room door, and it was opened.

Never one to shy away from the truth, I marched towards it. Just as I had last night, upon peeking inside, I gasped.

The hardwood floors shone, the rug on top of them, and the table on top of that. Nothing out of place. Except for Priscilla. A room-by-room search confirmed what I already knew. Priscilla was not here.

Her car sat in the driveway, morning mist clinging to the headlights, making them appear like teary eyes.

She never went anywhere with anyone, other than me.

Had last night all been a dream? But even if it had, where was Priscilla?

I circled back through the house, stopping in the kitchen. I peeled back the tin foil on a casserole pan in the refrigerator to reveal an untouched peach cobbler. I turned over my wrist. The scratches. The black kitten on my dresser. All of those things were proof. How had Priscilla's dining room gone from being a disaster area to completely restored overnight?

"Priscilla!" I yelled again.

In the living room, I turned around and around until I got dizzy, looking for any clues. After a few minutes, I realized I was so busy looking for what was there, I hadn't noticed what wasn't there. The white kitten.

I ran back up the stairs as fast as my knees would let me. In Priscilla's bedroom, the white kitten sat atop her chest of drawers. His smile was no longer genteel and serene.

I plunked down on her bed, unsure what to make of any of this. I did what I always do when I need to think. Chores. Since I was already there, I started with making her bed.

"Why, what's on these sheets?" I asked, drawing my fingers back to find them blackened. I rubbed them together and ashes flaked off, as I remembered the dragon from my nightmare.

I needed to call the police, but what on earth would I tell them?

Would they believe that the black and white kitten figurines were both possessed by evil spirits, opening up a portal to hell in Prissy's dining room? Would they believe that the dragon from my dream was real and devoured Priscilla, leaving only a handful of her ashes behind? That after he'd feasted upon her, he went back through the portal, which closed up, and her dining room supernaturally arranged itself exactly how it was before the whole thing unfolded?

Or would they draw the conclusion that when Priscilla McGibbon came to my house, during my favorite television show, drinking my tea and rambling about kittens, I simply could not take it anymore. I snapped, killed the scrawny little nuisance, and made up some cockamamie story so they'd declare me mentally unfit to stand trial?

Which would they think happened? Which do *you* think it was?

"What Happened to Prissy McGibbon"

KATHY RENEE JEFFORDS is an artist from South Carolina, in the United Stated. She loves music, hates being hot, eats more chocolate than she should — and says she is absolutely terrible at coming up with fun facts about herself that are actually fun. (We respectfully disagree.) She recently earned her first ever monetary payment for a short story, when she won 4th place in a contest hosted by *Postcard Poems & Prose*. She has never been happier to make $20.

She says: "Confession: I waited until the day of the deadline to sit down and start writing, so this story came together between me feverishly typing and complaining to my mom (and my dogs) that I wasn't going to finish in time and promising to never, ever wait until the last minute again (ha!). Usually, I have the skeleton of a plot before I actually sit down to write a story. With this one, I had no ideas: I just sat down and forced myself to add one word after the other, until I got to that last sentence."

Dig If You Will

"ONE THING WAS CERTAIN, that the white kitten had had nothing to do with it: — it was the black kitten's fault entirely." And she handed me back my iPhone with the cracked screen.

After that there was a stunned silence. On my part. She kept eating her iced lemon pound cake (free) and sucking on the green straw of her diabetic coma-inducing frozen confection? (also free — you're welcome, by the way.)

I stared at the photo again. And closed the tab.

And just sat there unblinking at her clinking braids and her Vineyard Vines freaking whale shirt.

Maybe I should back up. (Maybe I should try college again.) Maybe I should just keep going, 'cause that's what eventually happened, anyway. I'll back up.

Yesterday, there was this training. You know the one, because of that thing that happened in that place? Where the people were uncool? The brothers went to jail, for God's sake for what? Waiting for a friend? So the whole chain closed for the day so we could all be reeducated, which was more important for some people.

It seemed like a righteous idea, you know? But they didn't excuse any of us. No matter what your skin color was. No matter if your grandfather marched with Martin. I mean, my grandfather was Jewish, but he was there. And my grandmother, she was half Cherokee, and half Creole. She didn't march. She was too busy cleaning some folks houses in North Carolina right about then.

It was the right thing to do — the training. But we all kinda dreaded it. Because everyone likes to think they know, you know? That they have it together, that they cool.

No one wants to be that guy. The dumbass. It wasn't going to be me. But I also didn't want to be the token person they asked about shit. *Oh, how did that make you feel? Did that ever happen to you?* And they made it clear, we couldn't call in that day.

I might have complained to my girlfriend about it. Once. (Maybe twice.) (Maybe a little more than that.)

(Maybe, just maybe, I bitched and moaned and freakin' caterwauled for about a month between the thing happening and the training. Maybe.)

In the end, it was cool. Not exactly kum-bye-yah where everybody hugs and then it's a cult, but it was okay in the end. A bit shocking at times. But okay. Folks be trying. And we were all sorta in it together and that made it okay, like we all called the cops in Philly and we were NOT GONNA DO THAT AGAIN.

And we got there through a lot of role playing and goofy stuff, and also making up stories about what happened in these actual photos. In real life they were pretty innocent, but I guess they were supposed to really expose your inner heart and whatnot. So people saw all sorts of crazy shit in them. Like those ink splotches or whatever.

And my girlfriend, she really wanted to know what it was all about, I guess after all my whining, just saying, "Nah, it was cool," wasn't gonna be enough right?

Sometimes you are better off just not sharing, you know? So I showed her a photo. One photo. From the training. We had to look at it and say what was happening in the picture. And then we talked about preconceived ideas and what it all means and what it would be like to the "other" or whatever.

I told her, just tell me what's happening in picture. Seems like an innocent enough thing to say.

Let me tell you, we've been through some stuff, her and

me, right? Like not major stuff, your typical stuff, pregnancy scares that turn out to be nothing, and "Were you looking at him?" kinda of stuff. But also there was that time she was mugged coming home from work. I mean, nobody saw that coming. I sure didn't. I'm just at home chilling watching the game, and she calls and is like, uh, I got mugged and the police want me to hang out here and stuff, but I thought you'd, like, wanna know or whatever.

So I figured, OKAY, she doesn't need me to come, the police will get her home, but gosh, it was a shock and all. And she came home real late (real early actually) and slept in and we didn't really talk about it for a day or so.

Apparently, there was a gun. But she okay. So we're good. I mean, stuff happens. Coulda just as easily been me, right?

Messed her up a bit. And the police kept calling, wanting her to come down and identify the guy and all and she didn't want to — kept saying what if she wasn't sure and I was like don't doubt yourself, woman, just go down there and say who pointed a gun at your head. And then she'd cry and then she'd not want to go out that night.

So it's not like we've never had to deal with stuff. And then there was the time her mom had surgery and she had to go be with her. I mean I missed her, but she had to go do that, right? Her mom needed her more.

We were cool after a bit. I mean I just missed her and whatever.

But so she keeps bugging me to tell her what happened at the training and I mean we are sitting at the place so it's a bit awkward, but I'm like, okay you want to know? All right, here you go. Tell me what's happening in this picture.

The honest truth is that people see all sorts of stuff in these pictures, right? I mean some of the stories people made up — makes you wonder what they were smoking before the thing started, you know? Crazy stuff, like the owners forgot to feed them, or a kid knocked over the glass.

Or there's other kittens you can't see.

I show her this photo, and for real it's just two freaking kittens lapping up milk from a knocked over glass. Just one of the kittens is all fluffy and white and the other is witches-familiar black. Like a little black panther. Actually they told us, later, that they just photoshopped the color onto them — and in the real-life photo? They were both grey.

They were freaking kittens, right? Alright, now? That's how it ended. Over the kittens. So I guess you are all caught up now.

But before I go, I gotta ask you — Which do *you* think it was?

"Dig If You Will"

HILDIE S. BLOCK is a writing instructor from Virginia, in the United States. She lives with her husband, two teenagers, and a white dog and black cat. She has been published in *Gargoyle*, *Cortland Review*, *Literary Mama*, and elsewhere.

She says: "When I saw the black kitten/white kitten thing, it just yelled out *race* to me. And that Starbucks thing in Philly happened. I used to date a guy in the early 90s who lived at 18th and Spruce. I couldn't stop thinking, wait, there's a Starbucks at 18th and Spruce? This changes *everything*. I contacted the old beau. We are both looking at Google Maps saying *How is this even possible?* That, my friends, is white privilege. And the next time I'm at Starbucks, all the baristas are all shades of brown and I'm like, what would it be like to have to go to this training as a person of color?"

Appendix 1

Honorable Mentions

We received nearly one thousand submissions to this year's Literary Taxidermy Short Story Competition, and many impressed both early readers and final judges. In the end some good stories were turned away. The following stories all made it to the last round of selection. Keep an eye out for these writers. We're confident you'll see their work in the future.

Ian Ableson, "Darwinian"

Hazem Abu-Ghazaleh, "After the Tulips Bloomed"

Timothy Borella, "You've Lost That Loving Feline"

Heather Carson, "The Black Cat"

Ailbhe Cashell, "Black and White, and Red Herrings"

Annina Claesson, "Cat Burglars"

Brian Douglas, "Atoned"

Sean Fallon, "The Kitten God Heresy"

Angelique Marie Fawns, "Wog World"

Jenni Ferwerda, "Sugar and Spells"

Jonathan Fore, "In Shadows"

Meghan Franky, "Pansy"

Laura A. Freymiller, "Katrina"

Sarah Gardiner, "The Loss of Winning"

Elsha Hawk, "Charlene's Tails"

Natalie Hayden, "The Great Escape"

Carrie Hsu, "A Butterfly's Blood"

E.E. King, "A Morality Tail"
Isabelle LaPapa, "The Traitor's Secret"
Carol June Martin, "Windwords"
Sean McConville, "Stopping by Woods"
Kyla McDonald, "Fishing"
Jeffrey A Messick, "What a Kitten Wants"
Sean Morton, "Around the Block"
Linda Mullaly, "Cats of Bedlam"
Tommie Olson, "Level"
Ylva Østby, "Pink Daisy Wallpaper"
Jennifer L Porter, "Kitten Roulette"
Guy Preston, "A Catnap Well-deserved"
Elaine Ricci, "The Whole Kitten Caboodle"
Hannah Todd, "Mr. Snuffles"
D. J. Tyrer, "At the Kitty Kat Klub"
Katherine McShane Urban, "Desert Creatures"
Dale Venables, "Everlasting"
Sydney Winner, "The Ink That Sealed My Future"

This Year's Judges

Given the eclectic nature of the three opening/closing lines in the 2018 Literary Taxidermy Short Story Competition, and our desire for submissions to span genres, we assembled a group of professional writers and editors from all walks of the literary life. The judges for this year's competition included a poet, a playwright, a mystery writer, a speculative fiction writer, a fantasy writer, a young adult writer, a horror writer, and a food writer. They had a challenging task, separating not only wheat from chaff, but wheat from wheat, and we are grateful for their enthusiastic and perspicacious participation.

Catherine Barnett is the author of three collections of poems: *Human Hours* (2018), *The Game of Boxes* (2012), and *Into Perfect Spheres Such Holes Are Pierced* (2004). Her honors include a Whiting Award, a Guggenheim Fellowship, and the James Laughlin Award from the Academy of American Poets. She has published widely in journals and magazines, including *The New Yorker*, *The Kenyon Review*, and *The Washington Post*. Barnett teaches in the graduate and undergraduate programs at New York University, is a distinguished lecturer at Hunter College. She has degrees from Princeton University, where she has taught in the Lewis Center for the Arts, and from the MFA Program for Writers at Warren Wilson College.

Kelley Eskridge is a fiction writer, essayist, and screenwriter. She is the author of the New York Times

Notable novel *Solitaire*, a finalist for the Nebula, Endeavour, and Spectrum awards. The short stories in her collection *Dangerous Space* include an Astraea prize winner and finalists for the Nebula and Tiptree awards. Eskridge's story "Alien Jane" was adapted for an episode of the SciFi channel series Welcome to Paradox. Her film *OtherLife* (2017) is currently streaming on Netflix. She is a former vice president of Wizards of the Coast, the company responsible for the collectible trading games *Magic*™ and *Pokémon*™. She earns her keep as a corporate learning professional, as well as an independent editor with an international client list of established and emerging writers. She lives in Seattle with her wife, novelist Nicola Griffith.

Stephen Graham Jones is a Blackfeet author of experimental fiction, horror fiction, crime fiction, and science fiction. He has published in everything from literary journals to truck-enthusiast magazines, from textbooks to anthologies to best-of-the-year annuals. Jones has been an NEA Fellow, a Texas Writers League Fellow, and has won the Texas Institute of Letters Award for Fiction and the Independent Publishers Multicultural Award. His areas of interest, aside from fiction writing, are horror, science fiction, fantasy, film, comic books, pop culture, paleoanthropology, technology, and American Indian Studies. Jones received his BA in English and Philosophy from Texas Tech University (1994), his MA in English from the University of North Texas (1996), and his PhD from Florida State University (1998).

Holly Kowitt has written more than fifty books for younger readers, including *The Fenderbenders Get Lost in America*, *This Book Is a Joke*, *This Dance is Doomed*, and *The Principal's Underwear is Missing* (a brilliant update of PG Wodehouse's *Jeeves and Wooster*, set in a suburban high school). She also wrote and illustrated the bestselling LOSER LIST series, which has been translated into ten languages. She grew up in Evanston, Illinois and graduated from Brown University. A former editor at Scholastic Books, she lives in New York City, where she enjoys cycling, flea markets, and West Coast swing dancing. She spends most days writing and drawing in her art studio in Harlem.

Brian Parks is an American playwright, journalist, and editor. He lives in New York City and served as the Arts & Culture editor at *The Village Voice*, as well as Chairman of the Obie Awards. As a playwright, Brian has produced works that are noted for their dark comedy and fast pace. Best known for his play "Americana Absurdum" (which consists of the two shorter plays, "Vomit & Roses" and "Wolverine Dream"), his other works include "Goner," "Suspicious Package," "Out of the Way," "The Invitation," and "Imperial Fizz." "Americana Absurdum" was honored with the Best Writing award at the 1997 New York International Fringe Festival and a Scotsman Fringe First Award at the 2000 Edinburgh Festival Fringe. He is currently Senior Editor at *4Columns*, a website of arts criticism aimed at a general audience.

Michael Pronko is a mystery writer, essayist, and teacher, born in Kansas City, but living and writing in Tokyo for the past twenty years. He has published three award-winning collections of essays: *Beauty and Chaos: Essays on Tokyo*; *Motions and Moments: More Essays on Tokyo*; and *Tokyo's Mystery Deepens*. His award-winning mystery novel *The Last Train* (and the forthcoming *Thai Girl in Tokyo* and *Japan Hand*) feature Detective Hiroshi Shimizu who investigates white collar crime in Tokyo. He writes regularly for many publications, including *The Japan Times*, *Newsweek Japan*, *Jazznin*, *Jazz Colo[u]rs*, and *Artscape Japan*; and runs his own website, *Jazz in Japan*. He is a professor of American Literature at Meiji Gakuin University where he teaches seminars in contemporary novels and film adaptations.

Becky Selengut is a cooking teacher, private chef, not-so-private comedian, and a prolific food writer. Her books include *The Washington Local and Seasonal Cookbook* (2008); *Good Fish: Sustainable Seafood Recipes from the Pacific Coast* (2011 and 2018); *Shroom: Mind-Bendingly Good Recipes for Cultivated and Wild Mushrooms* (2014); *Not One Shrine: Two Food Writers Devour Tokyo* (2016); and *How to Taste: The Curious Cook's Handbook to seasoning and balance, from umami to acid and beyond* (2018). In her spare time she co-hosts Look Inside *This Book Club*, a NSFW comedy podcast with Matthew Amster-Burton that discusses the free Kindle preview — and ONLY the preview — of bestselling books, usually while sipping Pinot Grigio.

Nisi Shawl is an African-American writer, editor, and journalist. She is best known as an author of fantasy and science fiction who writes and teaches about how fantastic fiction might reflect real-world diversity of gender, sexual orientation, race, colonialism, physical ability, age, and other sociocultural factors. Her debut novel, *Everfair*, was a 2016 Nebula Awards finalist, and her short stories have appeared in *Asimov's Science Fiction*, the *Infinite Matrix*, *Strange Horizons*, *Semiotext(e)* and numerous other magazines and anthologies. Her story collection Filter House was one of two winners of the 2008 James Tiptree, Jr. Award. During the ceremony, she was crowned with the Tiptree tiara and given a plaque, a check, a pie, and a ceramic sculpture of a duck.

You, Too, May Become
a Taxidermist!

All of us at Regulus Press wish to extend our thanks and appreciation to everyone who participated in this year's Literary Taxidermy Short Story Competition. Your enthusiasm and commitment far exceeded our expectations — as did the *overwhelming* number of story submissions we received for each contest.

If you didn't participate this year and are coming to this collection of stories new to the idea of literary taxidermy, we hope you've enjoyed what you've found. And if you're a writer, we encourage you — the present reader — to become a future author.

Regulus Press plans to host another literary taxidermy competition, and we're looking for writers, both amateur and professional, to stitch together new and imaginative stories. The competition is your chance to get your hands dirty and join the growing community of literary taxidermists.

For the latest on the competition (and to learn more about the possibilities of literary taxidermy), visit:

www.literarytaxidermy.com

We all look forward to seeing what you come up with!

About the Editor

Mark Malamud is principal and manager of busymonster, LLC, a consultancy company focused on advanced user interface and design. His collection of short stories, *The Gymnasium*, established the idea of literary taxidermy. His novel, *Float the Pooch*, which pits David Bowie against Stanley Kubrick against a background of alien invasion, future sex, and Yom Kippur, is widely unread. He holds over 700 patents, and in 2012 he was the 8th most-prolific inventor of patents in the US. His current interests include shaving, dark nights, hasty conclusions, and vowels.

Other Books from Regulus Press

Telephone Me Now

An anthology of literary taxidermy based on the first and last lines of "A Telephone Call" by Dorothy Parker. Award-winning stories from the 2018 Literary Taxidermy Short Story Competition.

Against the Bar

An anthology of literary taxidermy based on the first and last lines of *The Thin Man* by Dashiell Hammett. Award-winning stories from the 2018 Literary Taxidermy Short Story Competition.

The Gymnasium

Nineteen tales of melancholy and wonder created by "re-stuffing" what goes in-between the opening and closing lines of classic works by Milan Kundera, Philip K. Dick, Thomas Wolfe, Ian Fleming, and others. Short stories by Mark Malamud.

Float the Pooch

Disco Rigido, charismatic kingpin of black-market libidinal software, spreads mayhem throughout the world for the benefit of an ancient extraterrestrial intelligence that uses life on Earth as a substrate for procreation; while Doctor Memory, a back-alley neurosurgeon dressed as a rabbi, tries to save what's left of humanity. A novel by Mark Malamud.